E. F. Perkins

Poems and Prose Composition

E. F. Perkins

Poems and Prose Composition

ISBN/EAN: 9783337370879

Printed in Europe, USA, Canada, Australia, Japan

Cover: Foto ©Andreas Hilbeck / pixelio.de

More available books at **www.hansebooks.com**

POEMS

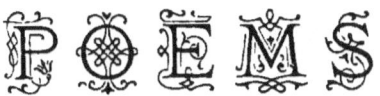

— AND —

PROSE COMPOSITION.

By MRS. E. F. PERKINS,

DENISON, TEXAS.

" 'Tis expectation makes a blessing dear,
Heaven were not heaven, if we knew what 't were."

DALLAS, TEXAS:
PEARRE BROTHERS, PRINTERS.
1886.

PREFACE.

I am, indeed, well aware that this book, like all others, will be subject to criticism, but I feel sure that in the great heart of the generous public (notwithstanding the taunted jeers of a few heartless critics), they will, in their just conceptions of imperfect humanity, make due allowance, and be more noble in their charitable feelings than to try to suppress so humble an one, for doing something hundreds of others have done.

And I hope when they view, these pages through,
They'll find the matter all original and true;
No flower of speech borrowed nor bought,
And but few quotations from others sought.

The most cursory glance over its pages will at once convince the reader that a number of these pieces have been written in various circumstances, only slightly differing in style. Otherwise often diverging widely from each other, and even in some instances two pieces have been written on the same subject with significations quite opposite to each other. This, as a matter of fact, may be readily accounted for by the peculiarity of circumstances under which they have been written or composed.

"Many men of many kinds,"
Make a world of many minds.
Many writers of many books,
With a figurative genius of style and looks,

Perpetually talk of its phenomena and power;
And in a flight of fancy they tower
Far beyond the true passions of the soul,
Into the mazes of a sylph or ghostly ghoul.

Time, place and age make a vast difference in writers' productions. In youth, when the mind and body are vigorous, full
of vivacity, exhilarated with the fascinating pleasures of future
hopes, the feelings, fervid and passionate, are unmistakably
delineated in their writings. But how different at the noon-tide
of life, when the mind and body have become fully matured, set-
tled down on fixed and true principles, on the real substantial
things of life, and can with the eye of age and experience look
back o'er life's panaramo of the past, and realize the phantom
hopes of ideal pleasures that are so animating to the youthful
mind swept away by living realities. Hence a marked change
in the writings of individuals in this period of life is observed to
be more grave and sedate.

But oh! how sweet, at late eventide,
To gather youth's flowers by the way-side,
When the silvery frosts of old age
Is mantling the brow of the time-worn sage,
When amid worldly cares and strife,
In the ever-changing scenes of life,
Beautiful gems of thought, like a sweet flower,
Awakens new life by its magic power.

Dear reader, in perusing the contents of this little volume,
kindly remember that we are but human, liable to err, and that
perfection is a rare blossom which seldom blooms this side of
heaven.

Therefore, be not surprised errors to find,
Not of the heart but of the mind.

MRS. E. F. PERKINS.

CONTENTS.

SENIOR DEPARTMENT.

PROSE DEPARTMENT.

10 CONTENTS.

INTRODUCTORY REMARKS.

PERHAPS, by way of introduction, it would be but proper to give the reader an insight of the different styles and composition, reflecting with fidelity the mind and spirit of the author, in order that they may better appreciate the different forms of expression used under varied circumstances, times and places in this work, as few can indeed clearly discriminate the real extent and importance of that influence which circumstances and surroundings have always exercised over human affairs, or can be aware how often they are determined by causes much slighter than are apparent to a casual or superficial observer; therefore, in justice to myself, I deem it of the utmost consequence to give the reader a few of the many disadvantages under which I have labored.

Having been reared in a country noted mostly for its broad area of acres and boundless, trackless prairies, inhabited by a bold, energetic and hospitable class of people who, like all other pioneer inhabitants, vied with each other who should have the largest farms and ranches, consequently very little attention was devoted to educational enterprises by our pioneer fathers until within the last twenty-five years. They seemed to think that

the wild, beautiful country needed development fully as much
as the population, for Nature's resources were then almost
unbounded for magnificence and utility. At that time the native
Texan was in the lap of luxury, so far as a primitive living was
concerned. Domestic education in that period of our history
was thought to be of more importance than any other. Our
stalwart sons and fair daughters were well educated in good
morals, industry and general usefulness, which is the only sure
foundation of a happy life. It is useless to try to build upon a
lazy, shattered constitution. If the body be depraved through
bad morals and stunted through inactivity, and the brain fired
and weakened through intemperance, the living principle of the
man has departed, naught remains save the shadow. Hence it
is very important that we should always have a sure foundation
on which to build usefulness and greatness

The youth labored under a great many disadvantages during
the development of our grand Lone Star State. The most prominent features were mental and social development. The first
was owing to the limited supply of the different kinds of educational institutions, and the latter from the intermixture of society
antagonistic to each other; therefore you will readily perceive
the different sentiments exposed in my writing. Sometimes,
prompted by a feeling of sympathy or veneration, perhaps
admiration, then my thoughts would flow out in that strain.
But if I should happen to see something which would produce a
feeling of ridicule or disgust, as a natural sequence my thoughts
would run in that channel. Hence, you see, by so many different associations, the mind is calculated to be detracted from its
usefulness or a more noble train of thought. Consequently,
amidst the many objects brought within the range of my contemplation, must, as a natural sequel, be the simplest and most
natural volition of the mind and feeling that has prompted all of
my writings, which requires neither for their comprehension

nor application any well-skilled philosopher to determine their meaning.

> Dear reader when these pages you scan,
> I trust you will be too noble a woman or man,
> To censure or ridicule so humble an one
> For doing what thousands of others have done.
> And when you view these pages with a critic's eye,
> Remember, as you try the mistakes and errors to espy,
> That they were composed and written by the hand
> Of one who was reared in the wild Texas land.
> A natural flower, blooming on her native soil,
> Impelled by no motive, save the upright honest toil,
> To say or do something to cheer the lonely way
> Of a friend, or reclaim a wanderer that's gone astray.

BIOGRAPHY.

——

In writing a brief memoir of my life, I shall only try to give the reader a few of the most important events or incidents that have happened to come under my general observation. In common with all other writers, perhaps it would be well not to depart from the general rule or custom of other authors, to give an insight of my ancestry. I am far from being in the least ashamed of them, for, like all other pioneer people who came to Texas at an early day, when the Indian war-whoop was scarcely over, as a matter of fact, they had to encounter many severe trials, and suffer many trying hardships and privations incidental to a frontier life, in rearing a family of small children.

My father, John F. Crawford, was born in the year 1810, in Madison county, Missouri. My mother's maiden name was Almira Zachary, daughter of Col. Caleb Zachary, who volunteered his services in the Mexican war, in the year 1836. She was born in the State of Tennessee, near the city of Nashville, in the year 1818, and spent only a very short time in her native State. My grandfather moved into the State of Arkansas when she was about eight years old, where he lived the remainder of his days. My father, also, when quite a youth, immigrated from Missouri to Arkansas, where he lived until he married my mother, in the year 1837. After five years of married life elapsed, he then removed to Texas, the Lone Star State, in the year 1842, equipped with a wagon, wife and three children, myself being the youngest, only three months old, when they reached their place of destination in Lamar county, Texas; hence I claim the Lone Star State my native State, as I was too young to know any other. My father's possessions were quite limited; his wagon and team, a flock of sheep, about fifty head, with some other stock, was his only estate.

This was, with their good health,
Their only happiness and wealth.
In a wild, trackless country, all alone,
Far from the old dearly loved home,
From friends in a distant land to roam,
With fearless hearts, among people unknown,
They built their cabin, fenced their land
With a willing and sturdy hand;
They soon made them a quiet little home,
Where love in all its purity and beauty shone.

But like all other early settlers, they were not content to live long in one place, but always seeking new adventures in a new country. They sold their few possessions and moved into Fannin county, near Bonham, and opened up a nice little farm, where they lived until the year 1850, when my father was elected to the Sheriff's office, when, for the convenience of his business, he moved to Bonham. In 1852 he was re-elected. At the expiration of the second term he became a candidate for Chief Justice, and was elected by a large majority. My father being a self-made man, relied chiefly on his own integrity and honest convictions as to what constituted a right or a moral obligation, and could never be swerved from the right sense of honor and justice to do a wrong to serve political party ends, or further some political scheme for the petty sum of money or popularity. The people soon found that he was a very conscientious man, that could neither be bought nor sold, but was faithful to the people's interest, who had given him their public trust. In the year 1861 he was elected Senator in the State legislature for the term of four years, but owing to the surrounding circumstances of his private family affairs, after two years' service he resigned his office and retired to private life. My father at that time had a large family, eleven children, six boys and five girls. I was the eldest girl, and had one brother older than myself. My three eldest brothers enlisted in the Confederate army in the year 1863, consequently all the management of the family affairs were then thrown upon my father to attend, which was too great a task and perform the duties of his office. So he resigned after two years service. Since that time he was earnestly solicited to become a candidate by his many friends to fill several honorable positions, but owing to his feeble health he did not feel like it would be doing justice to himself to enter again into campaign life after having served the public for twenty successive years.

There was scarcely a man in Fannin, Lamar and Grayson counties at that time, but what was familiar with the name of Judge Crawford, therefore it would be useless for me to say anything more concerning his public life, as they perhaps are more familiar with his public work than myself. At that time my youthful days, like most other girls of my age, was spent in the small frivolities of life, and my mind wholly absorbed in the glow and glitter of youthful pastime and amusements, took very little notice of the more important duties of life and its surroundings. My life then was like a happy dream that has vanished, that has forever passed into the shades of by-gone days, never to return.

My father is still living, but in feeble health. His place of residence is near Palmer, Ellis county, Texas. He was seventy-five years of age on the twenty-fourth day of May, 1885. My mother is dead. She died in January, 1873, aged fifty-two years, after a year's protracted illness of paralysis. Previous to the beginning of this paralytic stroke, she had always been a very stout, healthy woman, of a very industrious and energetic disposition, yet very mild and amiable with it. Both my father and mother have lived consistent Christian lives ever since I can remember. They were members of the Methodist Episcopal Church South.

I can scarcely realize my feelings when I view their lives back as far as thirty-two years, which takes me back considerably into the years of childhood, when I was about eleven years old, when life's early morning was gently unfolding its beautiful and precious endearments, like the tender rose opening its fragrant leaflets to the invigorating air and bright sunshine, and was not conscious of the many bleak wintry winds nor storm-beating rains that should so soon destroy its beauty and loveliness. Likewise in those beautiful years of innocent childhood, when my childish thoughts and nightly dreams were one of golden sunshine and happiness. Little did I then realize my precious opportunities and their value to the coming years. But, alas! perhaps this is the sad experience of nearly every one, when they look back on life's landscape, and see in the beautiful picture of the past the many sweet-scented flowers, crystal streams, bright-plumed birds and loved playmates, catching the golden-winged butterfly in the happy glow of youth. Then we can somewhat realize how soon the dark angry clouds can obscure the bright canopies of heaven, and the cares and trials of life how rapidly they throw their gloomy shadows o'er our brightest pathway that leads us through the dismal forests of the future. But in the lapse of years, time has not ceased to mark its changes, as gently down the placid stream of life we are—

> Rapidly drifting on her silvery bosom bright,
> To the eternal shores of golden light.
> Disrobed of earthly sorrows and care,

1

In a world more sweet, in a world more fair,
To dwell in peace forever there.
And though life's ills are hard to bear,
Yet, when over the surging billows wild,
We are tempest-tossed, a wayward child,
Methinks, he who rules all things well,
Will then our sorrows soothe and our fears quell.

As the beautiful days of childhood ripen into the years of maturity, time brings its many changes. Not unlike all other school-girls, I had my little troubles and trifles to contend with, such as staying in-doors and studying my lessons, and many other such trivial occurrences would very frequently happen. With the exception of these mole-hill difficulties, those were my happiest days, for then the world, with its false allurements and base deceptions, was a blank leaf in my life's journal. The more knowledge I have of the world at large, the more I am disgusted with it, for where I find beautiful flowers now and then, scattered by the wayside, I find many more briers and brambles; and whilst mine eyes are ravished with their beauty, and my senses delighted with their sweet-scented odors, my fingers are pricked with the surrounding thistles, which forces me to the conclusion that roses have thorns, and all "our sweets have their bitters." So among our few good things of this transitory life, we have many bitter trials intermixed.

Oh! why then so fondly cherish,
Transient joys that so soon perish,
Fleeting as the winds that pass o'er us,
A glimmering beacon light before us.
We vainly worship life's short-lived beauties
Too much, and neglect its more needful duties.

But he that doeth all things well, will always provide a way for us to travel life's rugged road, and if we desire to resist the great evils of life, make a way for our escape. I speak only for myself, as this has been my experience, and it is experience that teaches us the truest lessons of life. I presume that I have traveled the same road that a good many others have, and I am to-day not a lone wayfarer, but have a goodly number of companions journeying with me,—

To the haven of rest, that peaceful shore,
Where troubles and toils come no more;
But sweet rest, where the lapse of years
Brings no sorrow, sighs nor tears.
Oh! soon may time's barge calmly sail
Over the river on a firm, steady gale;
Safely bear us over on the further side,
Where with those we love, we can in them confide.
No hatred, umbrage, frowns nor jeers to meet,
But tender, loving friends to kindly greet.
Oh! let us make the very best of life,
For herculean time will soon end the strife.
Struggle on, has always been my motto, it can't last,
For soon our trials are ushered into the past.
And though change of scene oftentimes beget
Sweet pleasures, perhaps vain regret.

Yet it has a tendency to alleviate the sore distressed mind, and mitigate our sufferings to a certain extent, and may heal our wounds, but time nor changes cannot heal our scars. Probably, since I arrived at the age of nineteen years, I have encountered and persistently struggled through as many difficulties as most any person of my age and under similar circumstances, and have not yet ceased the raging warfare. I was kept in school almost constantly from the age of seven years until I was turned in my eighteenth year, when my happy schooldays were ended. Though not a graduate, I commenced teaching school out in the country. Those days were not in a fast age like the present, consequently I was no graduate, but only a good English scholar, for in that period of our educational history in Texas, people only had sense enough (they were such old fogies and mossbacks) as to really think that an education, like everything else, ought to be put up in a very substantial manner, built on a firm base that would be able to stand the weatherbeaten storms, and not wrecked by the bombastic prattle of bigoted fools, who are more witty than wise; therefore our teachers demanded a more thorough scholarship of their students than at the present time. A student was then compelled to be perfect in each and every grade of study before they were allowed to enter into a higher course of instruction; and, finally, had to be thorough in each and every branch alike, before they could be awarded a diploma. And when a young man or young lady received a prize medal in school, you may be sure they earned it. But now-a-days 'tis quite different. If students can robe themselves in a fine vesture, assume catch-penny airs, drive fast horses, with money to back them in their sports, it is no trouble to get a prize medal, whether they earn it or not, 'tis about the same as if they did, they get it. School teaching, like all other branches of business and industry, has undergone so many changes in modern improvements, that the easiest and quickest way of getting through, is said to be the best; consequently a smattering knowledge of the higher branches, with a little music, and a great deal of gas, giggle and courtesy, clothed in a fine habiliment, constitutes a modern scholar; no trouble to get his diploma and a newspaper puff, if he has the money, for that is the magic key that opens every man's door, and the only key that can open most of people's hearts in this age.

Oh! what a tyrant king is money. For the love of money, what is it people will not do? Oh! my God, thou only dost know, as it surely is outside of man's feeble comprehension. It

is, beyond a doubt, the giant king that now rules this sin-trod-
den world.

I can remember when our best school teachers had so many
old fogy notions about them that they really thought the
children could not learn to spell and read correctly, unless
they used a standard speller and reader. They earnestly con-
tended that the standard spellers and readers were compiled by
some of the most skillful and competent scholars, for the use of
primary schools, for the special purpose of learning boys and
girls to spell and read correctly. But our modern teachers,
with a few exceptions, have improved on old fogy teaching, and
have found out a better way. They can now teach children how
to spell and read in an arithmetic or geography; no use for
spellers and readers.

This is a fast age, and fast people live in it. An age of pro-
gression you may be sure. Boys are grown and think they
know quite as much as their father. Just as soon as they can
chew tobacco, smoke cigars, drink whisky, play a game of bil-
liards, and can read geography good, and understand mathe-
matics sufficient to stand behind a counter, and measure off dry
goods and weigh out groceries to customers, then they are grad-
uates. This is the class of persons that twist their mouth all
out of shape, and curl their lips with scorn, to call their forefathers old fogies and old mossbacks, who were born with more
sense than these young croakers will ever die with. I say, God
pity all such; they grew in too rich soil, it spoiled them in rapid
development, it dwarfed their brain. The bigoted know-alls,
who know nothing, are to be pitied.

I hope the reader will patiently bear with me in my oft
digressions from my preceding subject, as it has always been my
natural disposition to gather flowers by the wayside. I well
remember when I was a school-girl attending school in the country, my older brother and I had to walk about a mile and a half

across an open and beautiful prairie, interspersed occasionally
with those large thick-set clusters of wild roses and Texas pinks,
a deep crimson flower, which grew very rank in rich soils, and
hundreds of them in a very small space, which I thought looked
simply beautiful; therefore it was a sore temptation to pass
them without stopping to cull a few, and, consequently, I would
stop at nearly every place to gather roses and flowers by the
wayside, and most forgot I was on the way to school, when
presently my brother, who by this time was far ahead, would
call to me at the top of his voice to come on.   At once I would
realize my digression from the path of duty, and immediately
sallied forth into the old beaten path which led me directly over
the rising hill to the little school-house, with a firm resolution
that as soon as this irksome task of always attending school was
over, I would then gather flowers by the wayside to my heart's
content, and enjoy life's gay pleasures, if there were any to be
found, at all hazards.   But, alas! simple child, I was then in
blissful ignorance, for those were my happiest days.

> But years have intervened since now and then,
> The children have grown into women and men,
> Our childish thoughts and wily ways
> Of infantile joys and happy days,
> Have ripened into life's mature years,
> Through the varied scenes of sunshine and tears.

My last and happy school-days were spent in the Bonham
Female Institute, under the auspices of Prof. Solomon Sias, for-
merly of New York, with his four assistant teachers, Mrs. Sias,
Misses Clarke and Wilson, and Prof. Tryon, professor of math-
ematics, all from New York State.   They were very successful
teachers, but unlike a great many teachers now-a-days.   Instead
of killing time and getting their money, they worked faithfully
and earnestly for the benefit of their students, and were well

repaid for their labor by the high appreciation of their patrons. I left the school in the year 1860, about the coming on of the civil war between the North and South, when the turbid feelings of excitement ran high, and politics was the favorite theme of the day, and all hearts beat anxiously to hear the coming news, as our country then was on the eve of warfare. I well remember my feelings on hearing the first sound of the bugle notes and the beat of the drum, as our brave and gallant southern boys marched out to meet their own countrymen as their deadly foes. Yes, well do I remember those feelings; but words can never express them. Doubtless there are but few persons but what have at times those feelings. A kind of a passing strangeness seems to come over us, and our very soul is enveloped in a feeling of grand sublimity and one of awe, but inexpressible. Words are inadequate to express what we feel or enjoy. Oh! how sweet could we soar aloft on the pinions of imagination to the pinnacle of pleasure, where in the hight of bliss we might for a time forget our earthly sorrows.

Soon after I quit school I commenced teaching. Then I began to realize somewhat of a teacher's life and expectations, which were at that time something new to me, for I had always thought it must be grand to have the obedience and control of other people. Little did I then know how to appreciate the patience or forbearance of my teachers in their school-room duties, but I soon learned, you may be sure, as I had my patience fully tested. I must confess, I had more forbearance than I had really credited myself with, and I have always found through life ample means to meet all reasonable demands. We can do a great many things, that we call or think they are most impossibilities, if we are put to the test. But we often say, we can't do such and such a thing, when it is only because we don't have it to do, are not compelled to do it. If we were, we would soon find a way to get through, for you know that "necessity is the mother of invention." I can speak from my own experience, for I have been almost compelled to do things, and undergo many hardships and trials since I have had family cares to contend with, that I verily thought, when I was a girl in my teens, I could not do under any circumstances. But time and place makes all the difference in what we can or cannot do.

I taught school nearly four years during the war. My time being mostly spent in the school-room, consequently I had but little time to gather up or make notes of the passing events of the war times. I only kept partially posted through the local papers that I happened to get now and then, from which I gleaned a few items. I was teaching out in the country where mail transportation was not so good as it might have been.

I quit teaching school in the year 1865 to rest up a little, and I enjoyed the vacation immensely. I went off on a visit to one of my aunts, and spent two or three months very pleasantly. I formed a goodly number of acquaintances during my stay there, and had a great deal of amusement and pleasant pastime, as the city was noted for its good morals and love of literature, and, as a natural consequence, we could enjoy ourselves with more freedom than we can at the present day in most of our large cities. In our social gatherings, or even at public places of amusement, we were not compelled then with an eye of suspicion to shun the society of any one, but could have a rich repast in the way of social and intellectual companionship with any and all persons in attendance.

It was somewhere near the holidays when I returned home from my aunt's. Found all of my friends anxious for my arrival, as most of them were preparing holiday suppers and socials, for the benefit and entertainment of their loved ones, who had been absent so long in the army. After four long years of weary watching and fighting they had now sheathed their swords in peace, and buried the hatchet of war and blood-

shed, not as a whipped and vanquished foe, but as an over-pow-
ered and down-trodden people, whose sanguine hopes perished in
the lost cause, for the protection of their rights as free American
citizens, born underneath the downy pinions of the American
eagle, for they verily thought they were only trying to sustain
their dearly prized and bought liberties, purchased by their forefathers at the point of the glittering bayonet, the right to protect home and property. This they deemed right and proper, to
guard and protect their property, as they had paid their money
for it. They could see no justice in the people of the North robbing the South of her slaves, as they had been sold to her just
the same as any other merchandise, by men of the New England
States, who went to Africa with a little money and dry goods,
and took the advantage of the poor African mother's ignorance,
and purchased her children with a few laces, ribbons and other
goods, brought them to America, sold them into bondage, and
pocketed the money; of course. And when they saw the South
could utilize their labor to her great advantage and prosperity,
they then began to agitate a feeling among their northern breth-
ren that it was a sin to keep the poor colored man in bondage,
therefore he must have his freedom. They did not realize there
was any sin in slavery when the money was flowing into their
own pockets, through that source; it was all right then. If they
had realized, after so long a time, that it was a sin to have
people in bondage, and after having the use of the money they
received for the introduction and sales of them, when they sold
them into bondage to the South, why did they not pay us something for them. It would have reflected more honor, on their
part, to them. As it is, I see no honor nor glory in it, and it
would have cost less than the war.

But the war is over, and we will bury its contentions and old
grudges underneath the pillow of charity, and with the mind of
sweet forgetfulness try to remember no more past grievances, as

the majority of northern men were honest in their convictions of right. They claimed they were fighting to restore peace and harmony, and the union of the States, when in fact they were only riding a hobby-horse, put in by a few of the leading fanatics of the North to have men to fight to free the slaves.

But the war now I hope is ended,
With peace and harmony blended.
Let us join 'round the festal board,
With the friends that are to us restored,
To their dear ones and loved homes,
Where in contentment around it they roam.
But oh! see you those vacant seats,
As each one looks 'round and speaks
In loving tones, sad, soft and low?
Oh! how changed; 'tis scarce a year ago
Since those places were all, all filled,
But now they sleep, they were killed.
No more will their kind words greet us,
No more their pleasant faces meet us,
But from sorrow they have winged their flight,
Unburdened with care in robes of light,
They soar aloft in fairer worlds above,
To dwell in peace, in a land of love.
Then let us while in memory we cherish
Their last kind tokens, that can never perish,
Appreciate the dear ones more that are with us now,
For when they too have crossed the river, I trow,
We will then miss as much their loving smile,
And their kind words that cheer us all the while.
Wait not till a flower is faded and gone,
To cherish its beauty and fragrance alone;
But life's blessings now learn to enjoy,
For its present duties demand your employ.

Holidays being over, a lively reconstruction of business soon followed. Both boys and girls went to work earnestly, to contend with life's battles in the best way possible, and with brave hearts and willing hands have overcome many difficulties that seemed to obstruct their way to success. They are now enjoying the happy rewards of industry and economy in their peaceful homes.

Nuptial feasts, in those days, were no rare occasion. As a natural consequence, they were very common for several years after the war. I was married soon after this.

On the seventh of March, eighteen and sixty-seven,
My age was then thirteen and eleven.

Since that time my life, like a meandering stream in its windings finds its way through the cragged steeps, through brambles, briars and thistles, and flows gently through the flowery vale on its way to the grand old ocean, so my life has been like the winding stream, coursing its way through varied scenes, through barren deserts of hardships and disappointments, and occasionally through an oasis of pleasure, clothed in the most beautiful forms and flowers, that filled the atmosphere with their sweet aroma, which delighted my senses and thrilled my soul with the belief of a beautiful somewhere in the near future, where we can, in a sweet repose of forgetfulness, dream away our past cares.

MRS. E. F. PERKINS.

POEMS ✴ AND ✴ PROSE.

CHILD'S DEPARTMENT.

STEPHENSVILLE.

It was on a bright Spring's morning,
When bright Aurora was gently warming
The cool and fresh morning breeze,
Drying off the dew from the green-leaved trees,
That I my first visit paid
To Stephensville newly made,
By Stephens and his loved kin,
The whole family linked in,

To build a town of their own,
Where they could live and board at home,
Without getting far from uncle and aunt,
For any one else to visit, 'tis, " Oh ! I can't."
It was only last Sunday Uncle Hugh
Said with a smile, " Come over, oh ! do,
And see my new goods so nice,
For them I will sell at a low price.

"I have plenty of nice printed calicoes,
Ribbons, laces and fine hose;
To please the ladies is my aim,
And benefit my own individual gain,
For you must help to build our town,
If you do nothing but settle around,
Then you'll buy my land, and in my store,
If you wish, you can trade a score.

"Then, you know, it will be so pleasant,
To have our kinsfolk all present
At our little meetings in town,
And abroad, oh! how big our name will sound.
'Twill soon be, ' Where are you going?
To Stephensville town overflowing,
With pretty girls and new goods,
Wearing pretty dresses and new hoods.'

"Now won't that be nice and pleasant to hear,
It will make me outgrow my boots, I fear,
For you know that I am a little man,
With a big capital on a small plan.
And our town will be ahead of Bonham far,
Yes, it will be a long ways the brightest star,
For we are on this side of Bois 'd 'arc stream,
Closer to Jefferson for our team.

"My kinsfolk will do my hauling,
My hirelings can do my hard mauling;
Occasionally I will sell them a hat or shirt,
Or some calico, so their gals can flirt.
So now you can plainly see,
That I am certainly destined to be,
Among kinsfolk, a great man,
With a big store on a capital plan."

RAPID RIVER.

Flow on, thou rapid river,
　For on thy bright bosom
The silvery waters doth quiver
　As they silently glide on.

In thy bright reflected waves
　Heaves no anguish nor sorrow,
But in thy mild bosom laves
　Bright gems for the morrow.

O, that life would as smoothly glide
　O'er the tempestuous sea of ages,
As the gentle and heaving tide
　O'er the stormy sea that rages.

Roll on, gently in thy course rapid river,
　For on thy swelling bosom bright,
Gleams many a spray of shining silver,
　The twinkling gems of light.

NATURE.

The beauties of nature are seen,
In a little rippling stream,
As its glassy waters glide,
O'er little pebbles far and wide.

It is seen in a little flower,
When 'tis awakened by a shower,
Which revives its beauty again,
Till by some rude blast 'tis slain.

The beauties of nature are displayed,
By the orb of day in splendor arrayed,
As it throws its rays o'er the grass
Which absorbs the morning dew as we pass.

The beauties of nature are manifested
In the rain, as it forms its little waves crested,
O'er the little pebbles in the rivulets flow,
Onward bound a light doth brightly glow.

The beauties of nature are revealed
In the rumbling thunder and lightning's peal,
To arouse the stupid dupe, its mystery unravels,
As in the distant vale it travels.

SCHOOL DAYS.

Our school days are the happiest in life,
Free from care and strife,
Nothing to confuse the child-like mind,
Nor the thoughts confine.

But free and unbound we join in play
All so merry and gay,
Nor ever dreaming of life's sorrow,
But thinking of to-morrow,

And the many gay pleasures
And beautiful treasures,
That are stored in perennial bowers,
Counting them ours.

But those happy childhood days
Are flitting by like the rays
Of the bright effulgent sun,
To never return.

But whilst life's pathway we tread,
And childhood's joys are dead,
We will ever their sweet memories cherish,
Only with death will they perish.

SPRING.

Spring is coming with her buds and flowers,
And soon, with her sweet incentive powers
Will enliven all nature, her duties to perform,
And cheer the spirits of the weary and forlorn.

Hail, all hail, thou beauteous queen,
For over the coming year thou reigneth suprema;
To gladden old Earth, thou dost seem,
With thy gorgeous gems, the most priceless theme.

In both hut and mansion thy welcome is heard,
And in the forest, is proclaimed by the mocking bird,
Whilst from limb to limb, in joyous note,
He unplumes his wing, he dresses his coat.

And away he soars, his loved mate to find,
Who is ever the same, faithful and kind.
With joy we greet the merry, merry spring,
And with laughter make the forests ring.

Hail, all hail, the beautiful spring,
With gratitude in our hearts let us sing
The merry songs of love divine,
Whilst all nature in her beauties doth shine.

WHISPERINGS.

The low whispering winds are sighing
   A soft plaintive sound,
   Some mournful story have found,
To breathe on every gentle gale flying.

The green leafy trees their boughs are waving,
   With a solemn sound,
   Twirling so swiftly around,
You'd think them enchanted or raving.

The sweet-scented flower lifts its head
   To the gentle breeze's magic power,
   Then quietly in its rural bower,
Seeks repose on its lost companion's bed.

The merry songster warbles forth his song
   In sweet melodies on every gale,
   Telling his mate some love tale,
Which on the balmy breeze floats along.

The clear purling streamlets are flowing,
　　Winding their way through shady groves,
　　Unconscious of the rambler that roves
By its side, or the muttering wind above blowing.

THE PAST.

The past in bright visions ever lie before us,
　　Filling our hearts with sunshine,
　　And with all our joys entwine
Its beautiful garland of flowers o'er us.

Ah! the beautiful scenes of the past
　　We can never recall,
　　When sad disasters befall
Our journey, and o'er us its shadows cast.

Yea, the past is ever recalling by-gone days
　　To our wearied minds ;
　　Whilst to our hearts they bind
Joys, which through life are ever casting her rays.

How oft doth the transient joys of the past,
　　Rise in multitudinous clouds,
　　And in delightful rapture enshrouds,
The illuminated soul in a joyous repast.

Oh! the many sweet remembrances of the past
　　Are engraven on our hearts,
　　Till soul and body parts,
Then in heaven's bright clime they'll meet at last.

Ah! the beautiful scenes of the past are ever rising,
    And fast fading out of sight,
    Wrapped in the shades of night,
Will lie unobserved from the world's surmising.

OUR SAILS ARE HOISTED.

See, see, our sails are hoisted and flying,
And to the soft, gentle breezes are defying.
Soon, soon, this frail bark will waft us o'er life's sea,
Where cares and sorrows cease to be.
And though in different boats we embark,
Yet methinks I can see thee as a meteor spark,
Gently gliding on the mirrored waves of life's ocean,
To the sweet haven of peaceful emotion.

THE EMPIRE.

Our glorious empire has fallen,
    Fallen from her high estate,
    To share her untimely fate,
As did the late vanquished warriors.

Yes, the once great, glorious empire,
    That could boast of her power,
    And that she was the flower
Of the united world, has fallen.

Fallen from her high imperial throne,
  To one of ignoble birth,
  Which can never boast of worth,
To her sister nations from zone to zone.

But in shame bow her head to the dust,
  For in her raving madness,
  Hath clothed her land in sadness,
And with orphan's and widow's tears drenched her lust.

AN APPROACHING STORM.

The clouds are gathering thick and fast,
  The vivid lightnings gleam,
Whilst the sweeping blast
  Hurries everything into its stream.

Hark! hear her distant thunders roll,
  Reverberating through hill and dale,
Her dark and angry scroll,
  Shrieking aloud her furious wail.

The buzzards high in the air are flying,
  They sail 'round and 'round,
The storm's rage are closely eyeing,
  For they hear its tumultuous sound.

The storm has come with a leap and bound,
  Whilst its rain and hail hard is falling,
And the thunder, with her monotone sound,
  Drives away thoughts so fearful and appalling.

To-night, perhaps, some poor stranger
Wanders far away from home
'Mid darkness, toils and danger
To seek gay pleasure's happy zone.

————

WANDERINGS.

——

I have often wandered beside a little brook,
    Whose silvery waters glide
    In limpid streams far and wide,
Turning its way into every little nook.

And have often watched the golden morn,
    Bathed in streams of living fire,
    Brighten into mid-day, then retire
To gloomy eve and the shades of night forlorn.

And have often watched the last red ray
    Of the golden sun fade,
    And the silvery moon wade
The myriads of stars that compassed her way.

And have often watched the budding flower
    Blooming into life and beauty,
    And thought of our imperative duty
We owe to the great Giver of mercy and power.

And have often seen the little chirping bird
    Whilst building her tiny nest,
    Hopping and skipping, then to rest—
A mournful song from her is heard.

And have often seen the beautiful rainbow
　When, in all its glorious display,
　Disappears, and to misty realms fade away,
Which proves to us life is but an ephemeral show.

———

CHILD'S LETTER TO A FRIEND.

———

Dear friend, I write you a letter
To tell you that I am better
Since my pleasant dreams last night,
For, in my fairy, dream-like flight
I saw friends whom my heart holds most dear,
Their sweet smiles filled my soul with kindly cheer.

If we can not in the day oft have the pleasure
Of meeting, oh! what a momentary treasure,
To visit loved ones in the fairy dreamland,
And there in a sweet convivial band,
Join our harmonious voices as we are wont to do,
With the dear ones tried and true.

Forgive me, be patient and ever ready,
　A friend's infirmities to bear,
And in duty's barge ever be steady,
　Through life's rugged waves it will wear.

Though stormy cares around us gather,
　And sorrow's dark clouds lower,　　•
Let us in hope look for fairer weather,
　As our span of life will soon be o'er.

Good-by, loved one, remember me,
   Excuse my taxing your patience so long ;
May pleasant dreams attend thee,
   May you think I've done no wrong.

LOVE.

Who has found this precious gem sublime,
   That lives in harmony and hope of heaven ;
In his bosom a word of love doth shine,
   To him true happiness God hath given.

YOUTH'S DEPARTMENT.

SCATTERED THOUGHTS.

Scattered thoughts profusely lie
On memory's page 'till some passer-by,
Awakens them out of their sweet sleep,
And bids them their vigils keep,
'Till fond memory calls them back
To view life's bewildering track.

Scattered thoughts in fond memory fair,
How sweetly we treasure them there,
Like dear friends 'round our hearts entwine,
The living tendrils of affections caressing vine,
And oh! when life's shadows around us fall,
How sweet those beautiful thoughts to recall.

Scattered thoughts in fond memory dwell,
Of visions fair they oft doth tell,
When the sunshine of life's merry morn
Were clothed in their most beautiful form,
And though days, months, and years have fled,
Will be cherished whilst life's pathway we tread.

Scattered thoughts in fairy forms doth rise,
And bid us look beyond the eternal skies,
Where our dear loved ones are gone before,
Waiting for us on the ever-green shore,
Veiled in beautiful robes of white,
Basking in the glories of eternal light.

Scattered thoughts of the almost forgotten past,
Comes in surging billows thick and fast,
When around us the dark clouds lower,
And life's pleasures seems o'er,
Dispelling our shadowy forebodings,
And crowning us with joyful o'erloadings.

LINES TO A FRIEND.

Dear friend, when these lines you see,
In fond remembrance think of me,
Doubt not that absence can ever,
Though long it may be, our friendship sever.

And as you journey the weary way of life,
Though sorrows dark, and dangers rife,
Should in thy pathway profoundly lie,
Ne'er despair, but trust your God, he is nigh.

O come, cheer up, drive sad feelings away,
Let us look for a happier, a brighter day ;
When we can our dear ones meet,
In a world more fair, a clime more sweet.

And where troubles ne'er come nor clouds lower,
But the hard trials of life will be o'er ;
For the span of life seems scarce begun,
When lo ! we see its setting sun.

THE WORKS OF NATURE.

The works of nature with awe our thoughts command,
When we behold in them our Almighty Father's hand ;
For in profound wisdom were all things made,
The burning heat and the cooling shade.
The works of nature, how beautiful in them we behold,
Our Father's mercies for us wonderfully told.

The works of nature how infinitely divine,
All the beauties of our Father's work combine :
From the old ocean's surf-beaten strand,
To the fairest flower of our sunny land.
The radiant stars in cloudless heavens bright,
Beams softly and sweetly through the shades of night.

And yet, amid all the beauties of nature's works,
The grim monster of Death in them secretly lurks,
Destroying each with his untimely sword,
And with the fingers of time is printed on life's board.
Roaming around he spies every tree and flower,
And snatches them away in one short hour.

The works of nature, from them a lesson we learn,
That in the current tide of life the heart still yearn
For sweeter joys, more substantial and true ;
But like all nature, refreshed by the heaven's dew,
In the future hope ever blooms and fades,
Days of light and nights of shade.

Gentle breezes ever whisper the sounds of woe,
That seem to say you must soon yield to the foe ;
Soon Time will disrobe you of your beauteous bloom,
And lay you quietly in the cold tomb,
To sleep the silent slumber that never wakes,
Until the final judgment morn breaks.

———

GLORIES OF SUNSET.

——

O, beautiful is the golden sunset,
   Sinking to rest after a day's strife
   So emblematical of human life,
Likewise, man after all, pays nature's debt.

·O, beautiful is the golden sunset,
   When all nature is calmly reposing
   And her beauties fast enclosing
Themselves in dusky twilight's net.

O, beautiful is the golden sunset,
   As his last red ray
   Fades from earth away,
Gilding the murky clouds ere they met.

O, the beautiful sunset with tints of gold
   Glimmering on every lofty height,
   With thy beautiful golden light,
Art more admired than precious rubies of old.

O, beautiful is the golden sunset to me
   As I wander at eve alone
   Here around my beautiful home,
Admiring every spire of grass and leafy tree.

O, beautiful sunset so glorious and bright,
  After dark dreary days disappear,
  Like a sweet smile dispelling a tear,
Banishing sorrow in the shades of night.

O, beautiful golden sunset
  From our view art passing away
  Thus the closing of another day,
And soon life's sun like thee must set.

O, beautiful sunset so bright,
  How impressive are thy last lingering rays,
  Of life's own fast declining days,
That soon will pass out of sight.

O, beautiful sunset with silvery rays,
  Glistening on the mountain's snowy crest,
  Art softly and quietly sinking in the west.
O, thus may we end our halcyon days.

O, beautiful golden sunset,
  The radiant star of eve's decline,
  In splendor of a thousand hues shine,
Whilst thy brilliant rays are lingering yet.

O, the beautiful sunset's radiant glories,
  Reminds us of the golden shore,
  Where sin and sorrow come no more,
And heaven reveals all her bright glories.

HOPE.

In hope we rise,
  Far above the mountain's top,
And with tear-stained eyes,
  Our multitude of sins we drop.

SOLILOQUY.

I am now sitting here alone,
  In my room by the warm fireside,
Whilst my mind far away doth roam,
  To loved ones in whom I most confide.
Alas! on life's rugged billow,
  They are tossed to and fro,
Perchance some lie 'neath the willow,
  Whose lives no merit can bestow.

But on eternity's golden pages,
  Will be inscribed on its fold,
Many a bright sample of sages
  And ancient rhymes extolled.
The soft winds are sighing,
  But oh! my soul, how sad art thou,
As autumn leaves in sadness are lying,
  To know life is fading like the green bough.

SILVERY TONES.

Hark! hear ye those soft silver tones,
  Ringing loud and clear,
  Which to our hearts are so dear,
When in dreary solitude we are alone.

Yes, sweet are those sonorous sounds,
  As they echo through hill and dale,
  Flying on every gentle gale,
Wafting their sweet melodies all around.

O, breathe ye something to our hearts,
   That will soothe and drive away care,
   And make our skies once again fair,
O, breathe ye something that a balm imparts.

But, listen! hear ye those loud shrill notes,
   Chiming through the air,
   Perhaps tidings they bear,
Swiftly as the whispering wing that floats.

Hark! 'tis the knell of departing day,
   That steals along,
   Amid the crowded throng,
And soon, very soon to inanity will fade away.

THE FARMER.

Of all men, the farmer lives the happiest life,
With his kind loving wife
To cook his meals and milk the cow,
Whilst he steadily drives the plow.

He learns his boys to use the hoe,
To rake, to reap, and to mow,
To harness, whip, and to drive,
For without labor they cannot survive.

He teaches them trees they must fall,
To cut, split, and to maul,
To build, rake, and to scrape,
If they a good living would make.

He teaches them out of the farm
They must pack, stack, and fill the barn ;
To pull, bind, and to tie
Roughness for their stock, else they will die.

He teaches them all the rules of farming,
Its hardships, treasures, and pleasures so charming ;
Its name, worth, and priceless fame,
Which leads them to honor and not to shame.

He teaches them with their hands employed
They'll never and forever be annoyed
With vice, folly, and wicked sin,
But enjoy life without and within.

He teaches them useful knowledge to gain,
By sowing, reaping and storing grain ;
Thus slaving, saving, and making,
Will procure a fortune worth staking.

And with a little surplus money procured,
By locking, saving, and secured
From making, and taking the proceeds of the farm,
He sends his boys to school to " larn."

With cheerful and pleasant looks,
Their pencil, slate, and books,
Their pen, paper, and ink,
They are off to school before you can think.

And with a merry laugh they'll say,
We'll learn, jump, and play,
Reading, writing, and our fun
We will have, for our work is done.

SWEET MEMORIES.

Sweet memories are ever gliding,
  In visions bright;
Bringing the glad tidings,
  Of joys filled with delight.

Ah! sweetly doth memories of the past,
  Come flitting by;
And swiftly like a sweeping blast,
  Past us doth fly.

Yea, sweet memories like the golden sun,
  Her beautiful rays,
Around our benighted paths run,
  Thus illumining our dark days.

And like the soft summer breeze,
  We welcome thy stay;
Yet thou wilt our warmest hopes freeze,
  And fill our hearts with dismay.

THE PORTER.

When the porter let his orders fly,
There was a maiden with brillliant eye;
You know your State's namesake,
This broad hint you can but take.

Whose palpitating heart was floating high,
On sweet love's lofty wave;
Trying to ensnare with a heaving sigh,
The son of an honored brave.

3

But woe to the fair deceiving maiden,
For in her own deception she was caught ;
Deceiving one on whom was devotedly laden,
Her heart's love in beautiful words vainly wrought.

Take it to your heart, pine and repine,
The loss is yours, the gain is mine ;
The mountain which between us stands,
Was built by your actions, not with your hands.

Which can never be removed by a simper,
For this you know is not my temper ;
But of all things I love best,
I love you among the rest.

Of these, dried beef, a mackerel fish,
I choose none, for neither I wish.
Come now, collect all your wits,
Try the stocking, and see who it fits.

I THINK OF THEE.

I think of thee,
When the golden morn sheds her light,
O'er earth in lambent flames so bright,
Dispelling the gloomy mists around,
Which seems all o'er our land are bound,
Erasing the footprints of care, when
I think of thee.

I think of thee,
When the livid streams of bright mid-day,
Burst forth in all her brilliant array,
Lulling all nature into a calm, sweet repose,

Bids defiance to friends and foes,
And finds me ever the same,
   Thinking of thee.

   I think of thee,
When the sombre shades of twilight fall,
And in silence listen to hear thy call,
"Or catch one faint glimpse of thy gliding form,
As through the halls you silently pass on,"
And fain would hear from thy lips,
   I think of thee.

   I think of thee,
When the low voice of the gentle breezes around,
Softly are stealing with a solemn sound,
That seems to awaken the tender chords of my soul,
And fills my heart with rapture which consoles
My belief that you will ever through life
   Think of me.

YOUTH.

Youth, like the flowers of the field,
  Is swiftly passing away
To the realms of eternity, and there sealed
  Till the judgment day
Awakens them out of their sweet slumber,
  To arise in forms more bright
Than the glorious sun, and without number,
  To illuminate immortality as the stars illume the night.

Youth, thou art but a fleeting breath,
  Breathed, and quickly on the winds

Art borne to old age, nipped by rude death,
  And forever lost to earthly friends.
But in heaven's bright clime can meet,
  Where death reigns no more,
But in sweet accord join 'round the heavenly seat,
  Where sorrows ne'er come, nor clouds ne'er lower.

Youth, so beautifully bright and endearing,
  Is but a transient flower,
When in its radiant bloom so cheering,
  Fades, alas! in one short hour,
And wings its flight to joys more true,
  To a world where youth ever blooms bright,
Dressed in robes of a brighter hue,
  Ever to live in God's eternal light.

THE POET LONE STAR.

Who is the poet Lone Star?
  This is now the question in mind,
Who dare to excel so far,
  The common race of mankind.

Ah, I know his person, both his verse,
  He is a bright star shooting up,
Who is rich in mind, poor in purse,
  Looking forward to the golden cup.

He is bold and independent of scoffers,
  Scrutinizes every event which passes
In the vicinage of the diligent and loafers,
  He peeps into every corner, those reflecting glasses.

Calm and unassuming he reigns,
  You would scarcely know it was he,
Who gives touching hints so plain,
  With willing mind and heart so free.

To him human nature 's a familiar page,
  He reads on the sky the coming years,
And on the brow of the silly and the sages,
  Their incessant hopes and fears.

He walks in dreams of happiness and delight,
  Where all is calm and serene ;
When the starry curtains are drawn around us by night,
  Then Lone Star with an angel might be seen.

Whilst at home in blissful repose,
  His heart beats happily, his thoughts far away,
And for his lovely one his heart overflows,
  With joyous hopes while waiting the coming day.

THE FLOWER.

A little flower in its blushing bloom,
  Seems to say with words of silvery tone,
Yet we live, we must sink into our wintery tomb,
  To rise again when the spring trumpet is blown.

It is now the loveliest of all flowers,
  Brilliant, fascinating and charming to the eye ;
But as evening comes it breathes its last hour,
  In soft whispering prayer, and folds its leaves to die.

It was a pretty flower, though its life was short.
  Which only makes our attachment stronger,

For 'tis natural to cherish the meekest sort,
 Ere they die, for then they are with us no longer.

This flower bloomed in morn's delight,
 And withered in eve's frowning face,
When naught flourished hope began to blight,
 It blasted, and in mother earth found a burial place.

We are as the tenderest flower that blooms,
 And yet heed not at the warnings of nature ;
But in sin many of us meet our tombs,
 Wretched, despairing, sinful creatures.

Oh ! why not seek that precious gem sublime,
 Which lives in harmony and hope of heaven ;
And in our bosoms a word of love doth shine,
 To us true happiness God has given.

ANGELS OF THE EARTH.

The angels of this earth,
 Oh ! where are they now ?
They are in the halls of mirth,
 With love painted on the brow.

Oh ! what is pleasure without
 The fair sex to adorn ;
This sad world within and without
 To cheer the sedate and forlorn.

The angels of which I speak,
 Is the fair, the lovely damsel,
Like one from heaven she doth speak,
 To him who doth ramble.

It is loveliness which God
    Hath given to woman,
To cause man's foot ne'er to trod
    To nothingness and ruin.

THE WISH.

O had I some secret bower,
And be like the little flower,
That has all its sweet fragrance alone,
Having nothing to cause grief or moan ;
But like the innocent dove,
And the guiding star of love,
Ever be the idle pet of joyous youth,
Which is ever sacred in truth.

THE SETTING SUN.

In the far west the sun is setting,
    'Neath the golden robes of clouds shining ;
And whilst all earth is now fast jetting,
    The love of God around our hearts are twining.

How lovely all nature seems to be,
    When smiling eve doth come ;
When earth's rarest beauties we see,
    Tinged by the setting sun.

The birds gather and sing their songs so free,
    To the God who made the golden sun ;
And fly to the tops of the highest tree,
    To watch the setting sun.

All nature doth seem to adore and love,
  Rendering grateful thanks to God in one voice,
For that glorious privilege he doth us allow,
  In his light to live, in his love rejoice.

When the blushing sun is setting,
  When tiny stars appear in the sky ;
Then we are merry, our cares forgetting,
  Happily our time is flitting by.

Our cares the setting sun doth banish away,
  It gives pleasant thoughts and happy hearts ;
Whilst with us it makes its short stay,
  And for other realms soon departs.

GOD A LOVER OF BEAUTY.

When we view the works of the All-wise being,
  And see how beautifully they are formed,
  We can with admiration exclaim,
Oh ! what a lover of grandeur and beauty.
And what reverent soul whilst seeing
All nature in her beautiful forms adorned,
  Can with irreverence its author profane,
  Who has so kindly clothed our homes in beauty.

The wild old forest in forms of beauty he carved,
  Whilst there was no eye to behold
  The works so beautifully made.
Yet he formed them in grand sublimity,
For our soul's great delight, and starved
The tempter out of designs so bold,
  Who were about to invade
  This beautiful land of divinity.

Yes, God has made everything in its time beautiful.
  Every vine, flower, leaf and stem,
  Is a form of beauty, lovely and divine.
Yes, every landscape, hill and dale is beautiful,
And nature in so clothing mountains and glens,
Inspires within the minds of the dutiful,
    The graces of piety and love,
    Whilst beholding earth's duties sublime.

Yes, God has made everything in its time,
    Beautiful and lovely in form,
    Every diamond, rock, and pebbly beach,
Is a quarry of beauty bounteously laid,
Along the isles of earth, in rich mines,
Where many a pedestrian weary and forlorn,
    Strives their glittering diamonds to reach,
    And with life's hard struggles is poorly repaid.

LINES TO MATTIE—TRUST.

In my dreams thy voice is sweet to hear,
    Like the notes of a bright silver bell,
On the wings of imagination borne to my ear,
    Brings sweeter joys to my heart than words can tell.

Everywhere the same sweet voice I hear,
    The gentle breeze bears it along ;
The sparkling dewdrops glisten with a tear,
    When thy low voice awakens in song.

Oh ! ye that wander in love's charms,
Come hither and rest in my arms ;
And you may be content and sure,
That in my love you will be secure.

My dear, you and I must part,
In love I yield my heart,
To one whose bosom is like snow,
Pure, unstained from grief or woe.

PRAISE GOD.

Come, all that know the Lord.
Link your hearts with sweet accord,
And praise your Father, the God on high,
He will heal your sorrows and relieve your sigh.

Kind blessings on you he will bestow,
Which temptation can never overthrow;
Then let us serve our God as duty calls,
And rejoice in the blessings that around us fall.

A FOND FAREWELL.

My friend, ere I bid thee farewell,
'Twould be vain for me to tell,
The depth of those sweet, sacred ties,
That so near my heart lies.

For thy graces, like some fragrant flower,
Hath charmed me into love's sweet bower;
And in her cool and soft retreat,
Will ever be a place sacred and sweet.

When around me fall sorrow's dark shades,
And the bright star of hope fades,
There will I linger and think of thee,
And the many pleasant hours you spent with me.

And though from thee I am far, far away,
Yet thou wilt be in fond memory a brighter ray,
A vivid star on life's horizon which will ne'er set,
But will remain unsullied from vain regret.

And whilst here we wander in paths unknown,
We think of the happy hours that have flown,
And have forever passed from us away,
When life's pleasures were so bright and gay.

And though the dark clouds gather o'er us,
Yet methinks there's a brighter life before us,
A celestial world, filled with glory and sunshine,
Where the soul knows no sorrow nor days decline.

PASS THE TICKETS.

Pass the tickets around the room,
We'll have a smack, and jump the broom ;
Pass the tickets 'round by and by,
If you pass us we will ne'er sigh.

Come, open that selfish heart,
And with a free will let us share a part ;
Or close your scanty soul within,
And bury your love beneath your chin.

Beware of false pretensions, maid,
And of those whom you upbraid.
Thou art a criminal and his penalties shall bear,
Be on thy guard lest you a portion may share.

It is not in anger when we thus tatter,
But sad mistaken love is the matter.

We are often at outs, then together,
Now at outs, thank anger forever.

Come, think whilst reading this, 'tis you
Whom I address in lines so few ;
Think, you fungus-headed mink,
You know not what is penned in ink.

But you must not sink in despair,
For like other creatures, mortal we are ;
And our vows should not be broken,
Yet 'tis true, mortals are oft heart-broken.

THE FAREWELL.

Oh ! the dear impassionate sigh,
When a fond farewell is nigh ;
Breathes forth a volume from the heart,
To the dear one that is about to depart.

Farewell, may kind heaven ever bless thee,
And sweet joys ever caress thee ;
" May true friendship around you entwine,
Gems and joys of heaven's mine."

Farewell, may you never sorrow's pathway tread,
But in the enchanting arms of bliss be wed ;
May love weave its garland of flowers o'er thee,
And its sweet smiles ever lie before thee.

Farewell, my best wishes and prayers shall be
Breathed on every sighing breeze for thee ;
And when the golden sun of life is set,
Until then, only then, can I thee forget.

Farewell, may you ever through life remember,
The friend who now these lines doth tender;
To know they hold a place in thy affection,
Would be joy beyond all serious reflection.

Ah! 'tis hard to bid thee farewell,
Nevertheless fate decrees this sad spell;
And to her dominions we will have to yield
The wide domains of life's field.   .

MY LOVE.

Oh! my love 'tis killing me,
My tongue wont speak, my eyes wont see,
For my loved one is sweetly smiling,
Whilst loved thoughts in my heart are spoiling.
And I never could see for my life
Why the boys all don't get a wife,
For there's plenty of girls
With beautiful, golden curls,
To marry, would give worlds.

THIS WORLD A VAIN SHOW.

This world is all a frivolous show,
    Its pursuits are all vain;   .
The joys which to-day profusely flow,
    Are to-morrow succeeded by pain.

The grave, the gay, the young, the old,
    That so kindly join in mirth,
Perhaps to-morrow lie deathly cold,
    Consigned to the mother earth.

The transient joys that so soon pass
　From life's merry morn,
Are like the flowers and grass,
　Which in their prime are rudely shorn.

Yes, the gay pleasures of to-day
　Will soon pass out of sight,
And from youth's horizon fade away,
　To dwell in endless night.

Our fairy dreams of joy and pleasure,
　One moment they bloom and fade—
So flies to distant lands our treasure,
　And the debt of Nature is paid.

So speedily we are passing away
　To realms of an unknown sphere,
Where reigns in eternity endless day,
　For no night ever draws near.

O, may it be a day bright and serene,
　Calm as a bright spring's morning;
No dark lowering clouds to be seen,
　But all be clothed in beautiful adorning.

The golden gates are thrown open to all,
　But few reach that blissful place;
Their numbers are exceedingly small.
　Though many start, but few win the race.

"This world has many snares our feet to try,"
　The storms of sorrow around us roar,
But soon from their grasp we will fly
　To a land of bliss where tempests are no more.

So with renewed vigor let us press onward,
  For the faithful there is a promise sure;
But the heedless will travel the road downward,
  Where remorse of pain they will endure.

· ———

ANSWER TO APRIL FOOL.

———

Ah, ha! so I detected you at last,
I had suspicioned you was fast,
But thought perhaps I had better not say much,
For guilty conscience will betray all such.

And now, in answer, let me say to you,
That you will find me sincere and true,
Especially to one whom like yourself comes out so bold,
In words so beautiful their love to unfold.

But ah! like all other gay young men,
You will flatter young ladies now and then,
For simple amusement and frolicsome sport,
To make them think you are a fine beau to court.

But fie! with all your fine speeches I won't believe
You think every time the girls you can deceive,
If you do jest about blue-edged dishes,
For in the deep, deep sea there are many fishes.

And after fishing many a year, you may catch no better,
But in love's golden chain you may fetter
Some fair one, whose nectar steeped in hope's bright pool,
May never regret she got an April fool.

TEXALENE.

It was a stormy night,
  When I had a dream
Which denied me the right
  Of my dear Texalene.

Oh! my dear, my beautiful Texalene,
  "My love, my only love;"
In all my thoughts and in my dreams
  I see her form in climes above.

Her cheeks they glow,
  Her hazel eyes are bright,
Her form is far below
  The gorgeous mountain height.

Oh! my dear, my lovely Texalene,
  My darling and my pride,
In my thoughts, in all my dreams
  Thou art, in fancy, sitting by my side.

My beautiful Texalene is so gay,
  She is the pride of the vale;
Lovely birds around her play,
  And tell her a lover's tale.

Oh! my dear, my lovely Texalene,
  "My love, my only love;"
Thou art the brightest star in my dream,
  Thy voice is low and sweet as the turtle dove.

Thy sweet brow is so delicate and fair,
  Like snow when the pale moon is shining;
Thy head is clustered with curls of raven hair,
  Which around thy temples are twining.

Oh! my dear, my only Texalene,
"My love, my only love;"
Thy form in bright visions gleam,
    Like silvery crowned angels above.

Thou art like the golden winged linnet,
    That sings in morning's early hour;
And smiles each weary minute,
    Musing in the willow's leafy bower.

Oh! my dear and darling Texalene,
    My love and ambitious pride;
Thou art like a fairy in my dreams,
    And in my visions my darling bride.

Oh! my dear, my sweet Texalene,
    My love I cannot well restrain;
Of thee nightly I am sure to dream,
    With me till death thine image will remain.

The nights grow lonesome and weary,
    Every hour a day, dull and cheerless,
Except in slumber, then I am merry,
    All earth's enchanting scenes are peerless.

PAST.

In the back-ground of our hearts,
    Are the many cares of the past,
Which bring to view its piercing darts,
    On memory's wings thick and fast.
The past is gone, where, no mortal knows,
    It came and went and left no claim

4

For the future, but as the river, Time, flows,
  His victims are numbered in the battle of the slain.
He grasped the tender flower, as he went
  Over this sweet land of peace ;
He waged war, and many lives he spent,
  When death came his rage to cease.
The past is gone to the land of rest,
  To reign no more in supreme power ;
He shall never more our homes distress,
  For the present he submits in his dying hour.

PRESENT.

The present, 'tis here, oh ! what is the present,
  It is now the time all being,
Which makes the tide of life so pleasant,
  'Tis that all seeing yet unseen.
The present is with us now at hand,
  Ah ! he comes and goes flitting by,
As old past leaves destruction on the land,
  Then on eagle's wings doth fly.

VALENTINE'S EVE.

One day, before birds and fowls,
Maidens, as morning robins, mated with owls.
There were many behind curtains unseen,
Others in front, a fair sample of green.

Some walked, others played, the rest talked.
Ah! a gay time had they not balked

As they run their merry wits around.
One, with more wit than wisdom, found

A play called "Simon's Thumbs Down;"
So with thumbs down and up they went 'round,
Making themselves a happy evening spent,
With boys and girls in love full bent.

All had gathered there for the happy hour,
All a happy throng of the wedding tour.
There were babes to screech a tuneful air;
Infancy, youth, and old age were there

To cheer the bride and happy groom
Whilst leaving their fond, parental home,
To seek a new home, a happy home, a new life;
Once a beau, now a husband; once a maid, now a wife.

A REPLY.

Mr. Frank, in reply to date twenty-first,
    Let me to you a secret tell,
    And it you must remember well,
Not to plead bashfulness when boldness comes first.

And the beautiful blushing rose,
    Bears but a faint resemblance,
    To your pretended hindrance.
Oh! dear bashfulness, what? who knows

What lies hidden in that word? If revealed
    Would a volume of—I won't say what,
    For I know you care not,
But as an excuse, you say my fate is sealed.

And though my destiny were not sealed, yet I fear,
    My fate like yours would be,
    Bashfulness in the last degree.
Oh ! 'tis a pity, O sympathy, drop a tear

For two of the most bashful folks,
    You in your life ever saw,
    And always a distinction draw,
Between blushing roses and bashful folks.

WHEN I MARRIED.

I married in eighteen hundred and sixty-seven,
My age was thirteen and eleven ;
My husband in his prime, four yours older,
Made him look more wise and bolder.

Some months before we were married,
He rented a farm where we tarried,
Until he stored his forage and grain,
Then we moved our lodging again.

We moved into a little new house,
Were we lived snug as a mouse ;
Nothing to molest the quietude of our home,
But with contentment around it to roam.

Though cheaply built, planks set on end,
Through necessity we had no money to spend,
Rearing fine houses and making a show,
For we had to buy other indispensables, you know.

But in our little new house I sleep
As soundly as the king in his palace neat,
With no midnight haunts of vice,
To steal my brains without a price.

I reign as queen in our little domicile,
Superintending household duties with a good will;
Knowing that free labor has played out,
And hired labor is not worth having about.

So with sleeves rolled up, I visit the kitchen,
Nor slight the dairy, for there I must pitch in ;
Attention it needs, to keep it in repair,
To be in trim for other people's stare.

For you must know people nowadays,
Find, without a doubt, many ways
To sneer at the poverty of the poor,
Though it be loudly knocking at their own door.

And now riches has about "played out,"
Boys and girls will have to work beyond a doubt,
But 'twill be so fashionable they wont mind
Its name so much, but in it a pleasure find.

For I do assure you I am as contented
As most Mr. Anybody Else, and not repented
My making a choice in life,
For my husband is kind and I a dutiful wife.

With peace and plenty of provision,
What care I for other people's derision ;
For a contented mind, calm and serene,
Will with life's pleasures beam.

In climbing, I'll try to pull the right ropes,
In living, I'll try to live in bright hopes ;
For hoping is the chief sustenance of woman,
And always in adversity her brightest omen.

My evening's scribble is about done, for night
Is fast throwing her shades over my light,

As if to say, "Put up your paper, pen and ink,
For there's other duties of which you do not think."

Now, dear critic, when this you criticize,
Think not the writer did this your wit to exercise,
But merely to pass a little of your leisure time,
In laughing at my silly rhyme.

TO JENNIE.

Be assured dearest, that in affections budding wreath
  Thou art tenderly twined,
Being on my bosom's flowery heath,
  A favorite flower refined.

IMPROVEMENT.

"Stamp improvement on the wings of time,"
  In a nation's mighty career,
There's a chance for you to shine,
"Stamp improvement on the wings of time."

Ere this you are fully aware,
  In carelessness you'll be left behind,
To grope in darkness and despair,
"Stamp improvement on the wings of time."

With this mighty jewel on thy breast,
  You will the lofty mountain climb ;
Like a silver sword your name will gleam with the rest,
"Stamp improvement on the wings of time."

The duty of your fathers on you rest,
  Now this consider with dutiful mind,
And with this motto ever be blest,   `
"Stamp improvement on the wings of time."

Mark the falling of great generations,
  Stamp the seal of remembrance in thy mind.
Hark! take note, 'tis the cry of all nations,
"Stamp improvement on the wings of time."

Stamp the seal that links the heart,
  To the love of all mankind;
Never, no never, from this motto depart,
"Stamp improvement on the wings of time."

Be an advocate of knowledge to gain,
  Mark the notes as the school-bell chimes
Speak the words clear and plain,
"Stamp improvement on the wings of time."

In thy youth to knowledge turn,
  With its contents store your mind;
For treasures of bliss it will return,
"Stamp improvement on the wings of time."

Thou art a shrub that bears no flower,
  Not as the stately pine,
The king of the forest crowned in power,
"Stamp improvement on the wings of time."

Rouse your ambition and manly courage, try
  To be a man of rank in the public mind;
With thy name exalted to the sky,
"Stamp improvement on the wings of time."

To climb the silvery mountain of fame,
  You must one thing bear in mind,

Never think learning a disgrace or shame,
"Stamp improvement on the wings of time."

It is a height which but few pilgrims reach,
   That lofty station of mankind ;
With those beneath them to teach,
"Stamp improvement on the wings of time."

Arouse ye, O sons of liberty, stand,
   Ye sons of the southern clime ;
Seize the gem with a deathless grip of hand,
   And " stamp improvement on the wings of time."

THE DRIZZLING RAIN.

The drizzling rains are falling,
And to our minds are recalling,
Sweet remembrances of the past,
Which, like the roses, soon blast.

Yes, the gentle rains of to-day,
Seem to sweetly say,
Behold how gently we are passing by,
Soon your years, like us, will have flitted by.

Yes, the gentle rains are softly descending,
All nature to their bland sway is bending ;
So we, like them, will soon travel the road,
That leads to our sure and final abode.

The rain-showers of to-day,
Will, like the flowers, soon pass away ;
And the dim traces they leave behind,
Will, like our faults, fade from the mind.

Though to-day the rain falls from on high,
To-morrow low on the ground doth lie ;
So the monarch to-day in all his glory stands,
Perhaps to-morrow grim Death his fame demands.

The driveling rain which falls to-day,
In gentle drops will soon wash away
The loose sands from every quarry beach,
So life, by Time's hand her destiny soon will reach.

DEDICATED TO L. E. P.

In the year eighteen hundred and sixty-seven,
    December the twenty-first day,
    Was born a bright little ray,
An angel from above to earth given.

But alas! its sweet little reign,
    Was soon on earth ended,
    And to a brighter clime ascended,
Where is known no death nor pain.

On the eleventh of June, eighteen hundred and sixty-nine,
    Aged seventeen months and twenty days,
    Departed from earth all its bright rays,
To heaven a purer and brighter clime.

MORNING OF LIFE.

The morning of life, like the sun
    In its daily revolution,
Soon its appointed course doth run,
    In time's ceaseless evolution ;

Then let us our precious moments improve,
    Lay something up in store,
For the noon-tide life will behoove
    Labor's earnest efforts more and more,
To prepare for life's wintery age,
    When the silvery hairs are thin,
And the pulse of the time-worn sage
    Beats slow, while the eyes grow dim.

A CONGRATULATION.

May your future ever be as bright
    And joyous as the present is ;
May gloomy sorrow ever wing her flight,
    Far away from thy connubial bliss.

May your pathway be strewn with love's sweet flowers
    May your highest idea of supreme felicity,
    Fancied in sweet hymeneal bowers,
Always prove sincere in honest simplicity.

May your glittering day-dreams of life,
    Be realized in this your happy consummation
Of gaining a true and loving wife,
    Whose sweet smiles will ever be to you a consolation.

May heaven's choicest blessings be with thee,
    And in life's garden ever bloom,
The joys which on love's altar are free,
    From vain mistrust and direful gloom.

May cares and sorrows as they meet you disappear,
    May your cloudless skies of love
Never be overshadowed by the midnight haunts of fear,
    But be as bright as the glorious sun above.

May your life be one of successive joys,
  Smoothly gliding on through a happy vale,
Gemmed by the dewdrops of love which decoys,
  Into repose and forgetfulness of sorrow's wail.

May you soon forget and forgive,
  The faults of your kind friends,
Who for a little sport, certainly did give
  A few practical jokes which never offend.

· LOVE DREAM.

Ah ! love is a sad sweet dream,
  That turns day into night ;
It is like a falling, trickling stream,
  Whose silvery waters gleam in every light.

Love is as a mighty king,
  It rules this glorious land,
And proves a reptile sting,
  When taken by the hand.

My heart glows with fond anticipation,
  Whilst I am thinking of my beloved one ;
The fairest flower of all earth's creation,
  With no exception, not one.

Her lovely cheeks, her brilliant eye,
  When evening spreads her enchanting shades,
Shows hues of every gorgeous dye,
  And with her charms, beauty fades.

I hope we will part but for a season,
  Think me not mad, on meeting I'll give my reason,
For it would give my heart great pain,
  To think we would ne'er meet again.

THE MAID.

I once loved a beauteous maid,
   I went to see her often too,
When alas! the fair maiden bade
   Me come no more, a farewell adieu.

Her form was beauteous to behold,
   Her eyes sparkled, her face was fair,
And her countenance unmistakably told
   The moment her love was there.

But ah! one day there came
   Beaux numbering one, two, three and four;
Now you have the number, not the name,
   Of the one that came before.

I am now called her present lover,
   Hoping to win her heart;
If I fail, mine eyes I'll cover,
   And from this unhappy world depart.

I love her charmingly well,
   With her modest feature,
'Tis more than words can tell,
   Ah! the lovely creature.

BROKEN-HEARTED.

Hark! hear you her sorrowful cries,
   Calling on one whose heart is as stone;
See the drops of grief gushing from her eyes,
   Her voice grows faint, her happiness is gone.

Her fair hand was wooed and won
  By a youth of her playmate days,
A sister's pet, a fond mother's son,
  But alas ! now how changed are his ways.

Her warm and tender heart,
  Has melted within her loving bosom ;
She smiled and wept when they parted,
  Shrinking back into love's cruel prison.

And in this unholy land of care,
  She lingers her untimely life away ;
The siren song of love to her proved a snare,
Her happiness to grief, an unfortunate prey.

To her, love's young dream is o'er, and alas !
  Hopes from her bosom have forever fled ;
And ere the days of absence can pass,
  Love shall prove withered and dead.

In her visions fair, her brightest joys have fled,
  All to her is a world of despair and gloom ;
She may now well lay that crested head,
  And hang that broken heart o'er the tomb.

WOOING.

Fie ! you may talk of wooing
  Widow's hearts.
And their bewitching smiles outdoing
  Cupid's darts.

But ah ! could I always have the pleasure
  Of seeing and sitting,

By one whose soft glances I deem a treasure,
    Ever past me flitting,

I would care not for a young widow's glances,
    Nor the smile,
Which you say her charms so enhances
    All the while.

No, but when the golden sun sinks
    Out of sight,
And the gentle evening zephyr links
    Her fate with the night.

O, let me be close by the side of one
    Whose dark eye,
And golden hair like the brilliant sun,
    Will never die.

But ever live green in remembrance,
    For her fair form,
There's but few that bear resemblance,
    Save bright morn.

But ah ! vague suspicions rise,
    For another seeks
To rob me of my expected prize,
    In a few weeks.

Whilst I have been for many months striving
    To win the race,
And thought my suit too finely thriving,
    To fall apace.

But ah ! faint heart ne'er won fair lady,
    Nor a jewel ;
And though my chance may be dark and shady,
    I'll try a renewal.

Ah ! for those bright eyes and golden hair,
    In wavy tresses flowing ;
I soon would to dry goods prove a snare,
    Only drugs could have a showing.

A BOY'S COURTSHIP.

I went out a courting one day,
All very fine and gay ;
I had to ride but three miles,
Until I reached her honey smiles ;
My steed traveled at a pretty rate,
Soon he landed me at the gate.

And there sat my darling in full dress,
I caught her 'round the neck, to press
Her ruby lips, so sweet, to mine.
She gave me a loving sign ;
I sighed, and leisurely leaned back,
Our lips going smicky smack.

And her papa, just about that time,
Slowly stepped up from behind,
Said, "Wretch, ungrateful daughter,
Bring your papa some cool water."
I tried hard to raise a conversation,
When the toe of his boot said, "Emancipation !"

I tried with him the case to reason,
But the old man said it was out of all season.
So then what do you reckon I did,
Why, right over the fence, without a shirt, I slid,
Falling into a large box of mortar,
Forgetting the old man's lovely daughter.

I piteously cried for some one to help,
And the first thing I felt,
Was the old man's leather strap,
Over my head going spat, spat,
I scrambling up to the old man said,
"O, pray, have mercy on this silly head,

For if ever I get out of this bad scrape,
I never will another such a trip make."
He, looking angrily to me, said,
"No, you can never my daughter wed,
And the sooner you my premises leave,
For the less you will have to grieve.

So, raising my hat, with a low bow,
I bid him good morning, as well as I knew how.
So that fatal but lucky blunder,
Cut my love for girls asunder;
And an old bachelor I have lived to be,
And the faults of boyhood days plainly see.

MORNING THOUGHTS.

Though the morning looks beautifully bright,
   With the golden sun just rising,
In all his brilliant splendor so light,
   Yet a dim cloud shrouds my soul in sad surmising.

But like autumnal showers
   Drown the emaciated leaves of decay,
And prepare the rural bowers,
   For brighter hopes of another day.

Perhaps those shady clouds of sorrow,
  Will but tranquillize the soul,
For brighter gems of the morrow,
  And sweet joys untold.

Though life's stormy cares 'round us gather,
  And sorrow's dark clouds lower,
Let us in hope look for fairer weather,
  For the span of life will soon be o'er.

MY GUEST.

Oh! I had such a pleasant guest last night,
You ought to have seen the sight,
He was so interesting and gay,
You'd almost thought him a twittering jay;
You have no idea the amount of bombastic prattle
He displayed in high-flown verbal battle.

His canting words impress my mind
  Like the ivy 'round the unyielding oak,
With sweet embraces her boughs intertwined,
  A reciprocation from him doth vainly invoke.

But with all her endearing charms combined,
  He remains inflexible, not swayed by her power,
But as a felon securely by his foe confined,
"Gives way but in his dying hour."

So his flattering words are vainly spent,
  For I, like the unbending oak,
Will never yield, nor be easily bent,
  By his various and untimely strokes.

5

KISSES.

———

Kisses, like the dewdrops on a rose,
   But a moment of bliss they enjoy,
Before its beauties enclose,
   Its floral sweetness to destroy.

———

MATRIMONY.

———

Matrimony is a life card,
   And when it does not turn trumps,
'Tis sure to make life hard,
   Fills its road full of ugly stumps.

But what a pleasure 'tis to ride,
   O'er life's turbulent sea;
In flying colors sail o'er the tide,
   To anchor on some beautiful lea.

———

WISDOM.

———

For but few doth wisdom's pages unfold,
Its mysteries lie in heaps untold;
How oft doth the unwary lad sing,
Of brightest joys which wisdom brings.

'Tis that thrilling in our bosom when we feel,
The tender chords of love grow stronger,
And in our hearts the spark conceal,
Till at last we can restrain no longer.

MEETING.

Dear friend, it seems so long since we met,
But you know 'tis often said,
That seldom visits ne'er cause vain regret,
But make lasting friends well bred ;
Yet methinks, lasting comrades or not,
It makes glad hearts not soon forgot.

O 'tis sweet to gather in a social group 'round
True friendship's holy shrine,
Where alone sacred love is always found
Its loving tendrils around the heart to entwine ;
Soothes our sad changes, brightens our dark days,
And fills our souls with heaven's bright rays.

MISTAKEN LOVE.

Notwithstanding the many pleasant hours,
We have spent in hymeneal bowers,
And the many kindred ties of friendship that in flowers
Were linked together, as we vainly thought,
By the golden chain of love, are by nought
Broken, yea they are forever wrought,

Never again in fancy to be reunited ;
So let each of us bury our love-blighted
Hopes, in the dark depths of oblivion, never to be sighted,
And remember the past no more, for to remember,
Would irritate a passion which would engender
A life of hopeless misery, without a defender.

Therefore, I beg you, never to think of me again,
And consider our affair mere fancies of the brain ;
The past only visionary, dreamings of love in vain.
Though they be not easily erased from the mind,
Yet the effacing fingers of ceaseless time,
Will doubtless ere the vital spark be resigned,

Obliterate it from the affections of the heart,
Though it be susceptible of keen emotion, yet when seared with
    a dart,
From the cold vauntings of unrequited love, shares no part
In the flatteries of life, but becomes heedless and insensible
To the vain promptings of delusion, which are incomprehensible,
Thereby shielding herself from calamities though not apprehen-
    sible,
That often makes broken hearts bathe in tears,
Yet for you I am not alarmed, for your credulity appears
Too sensible to indulge in a passion, which for years
Failed to meet a due return from the object of admiration,
Yet through the ever-changing years of the future, an altercation,
You say, may be wrought in my mind, and a final consummation

Be effected, through the angelic influences of tender sympathies,
Whilst in the deep recesses of my soul all the energies
Will call forth a compassionate feeling which, in its indulgencies
People often say transforms itself into ardent love ;
But let me entreat you not to be thus led on far above
Reason, by the mere phantom of hope, though the turtle-dove,

You say, is worthy of imitation, yet her constancy
She does not assume to that extent of your world-wide romancy,
For you are led on by vain imagination and puerile fancy.
And now I beg you to abandon your vain pursuit,
Fruitless will be your efforts and your honor disrepute,
For when I deliberately decide a question, I will not confute

My honest decision, unless fully convinced of an illusion,
Of which there's no probability, and it is a vain intrusion
To assert a right from mere fancy ; and now in conclusion,
Let me say that I regard you a friend, one that is true,
But nothing more, and I'll bid you a kind adieu,
Hoping this affair you will never want to renew.

OUR DUTY.

Oh ! who could forget God and their duty,
Seeing old Earth clothed in her beauty ;
And around her the all-glorious display,
Of the beautiful bright monitor of the day.

And after gloomy hours and dark days,
How sweet are the beautiful rays
Of the bright star of hope, as she ascends
Life's shadowed horizon her sweetest joy lends.

FANCIES OF LOVE.

O, ye soft sighing winds of eve,
Waft to me something sweet to retrieve
Of the past, but quickly flown hours,
When amidst friends and sweet flowers,
I passed my leisure moments so happily,
Nor ever dreaming of life's cares so drearily.

But alas! alas! how vain are our chidings,
Whilst life's ever-sure tidings
Bear us swiftly onward o'er its surging billows,

And at night when softly reclining on our pillows,
How oft doth sweet memories crowd our brain
With visions of past pleasure and pain.

Yet, oh yet, I will hope for the best,
If by happiness I am ne'er blest,
And if sad misfortune should e'er caress me,
And thy sweet smiles should ne'er bless me,
O, let me live in hope, if I die in despair,
And fly to some far-off region more fair.

———

IT WAS IN MY MIND.

———

There is a lass, all know her well,
As a friend I loved her, I loved her so kind,
There are many wise, but none can tell,
    It was in my mind.

I visited her, and the sight made me glad,
I remained all night, but it was a cooling time,
Though I loved her so well, yet she grew mad,
    It was in my mind.

It was a balmy eve, when last we met
We parted, either she or I was left to pine
One or the other, a heartless coquette,
    It was in my mind.

She did not rank with the higher,
But as a gee-gaw in her prime,
The idol of an inspiring squire,
    It was in my mind.

The star of her circle, in her estimation,
A dreg for me of an inferior kind,
A mock of the whole female creation,
    It was in my mind.

Now, dear friends, when this you read,
Commit the moral of this to your mind,
For absent minds lose their friends by careless deeds,
    It was in my mind.

A GENT AND HIS DINNER.

To dinner a Gent sat down, on looking around,
    He spied his favorite dish,
      'Twas neither potatoes nor fish,
But a chicken cooked nicely and brown.

Opening wide his eyes, said he, "This was intended for me."
    "Yes," said the lady, "'tis for you."
    Now quickly to him the dish he drew,
And carved the chicken into pieces three.

Saying, "It is very poor, they've starved it sure;
    The country folks don't mind,
    Anything of this kind,
They'd half starve themselves a dime to secure."

Then, with an air of pride he pushed it aside,
    His lips quivering like a leaf,
    Said, "Waiter, pass me some roast beef."
'Twas passed, not roasted, but nicely fried.

This not pleasing his taste, he went off in haste,
    Saying, "I do not feel well to-day,
    The poor chicken took my appetite away,
And think myself excused, as 'tis a save and not a waste."

TEMPERANCE CALL.

Come my friends, one and all,
And hear the grand temperance call,
Come and join the temperance band,
We will hoist our flag throughout the land.
Dare do right, no matter what people say,
We will drive, gin, rum, and whisky away.

O, think young man, ere 'tis too late,
Yea, act for yourself, ere stern fate
Shall the final destiny of your life seal;
O, then let it not be a vile drunkard's deal,
But a noble man, who will dare do right,
No matter how long, nor hard the fight.

So come to the front and take your place,
Fall in ranks and help redeem your race
From the accursed crimes, and sin
Of drinking whisky, rum, and gin,
"For who hath sorrow and woe,
Who hath red eyes without a foe,
They that tarry long at wine,"
Those who with drunkards sip and dine.

Remember what the great philosopher said,
"Look not upon the wine when 'tis red,
When it giveth its color in the cup,"
Oh, do not then, of its deadly poison sup,
For " when it moveth itself aright,
'Tis then like a serpent it doth bite,"
It stingeth, it stingeth like an adder,
It bringeth you down on life's ladder,
To the lowest steps of shame and disgrace,
From whence you can never your footsteps retrace.

Now, young man, ponder a moment and see,
If in this catalogue of evils you think there be
Anything desirable, admirable, congenial, or nice,
That will answer life's purposes or suffice
To throw, instead of shadows, a sunlight glow,
O'er the somber shades that gather around our door.

Then, oh then, shun those dens of vice,
That steal your money and brains without a price,
For the green-eyed monster has his winning way,
To ensnare those whom he intends his prey ;
With his skillful art, the unsuspected youth,
Ere he realizes the fearful consequences and truth,
Is in his iron grasp securely bound ;
No more will he heed the signal sound,
Given by friends to warn him of danger,
He now to their entreaties becomes a stranger.

Don't delay, join the cold water army now,
Ever, ever, to its crystal shrine bow,
Set our sails, unfurl our banners, let them fly,
Soon our bark safely anchored in harbor will lie,
Whilst our motto shall ever be, "Don't Falter,"
But drink, ever drink, clear sparkling water.

MY FRIEND.

My friend, it is with pleasure that I take my pen,
To write you a few lines, and in them
You will find something that you are not aware,
But please, when you read them, do not declare
I am poking fun at you this time;

For I assure you it would be hard to find
A friend who speaks so positive and plain,
And by no means exhibit any name.

But let me tell you one thing in fact,
And that is, without any tact,
You are the best looking one of your mess,
In plain speaking, and without any jest.
Now, don't think I'm flattering you,
For that would be the last thing I'd do ;
And I'm sure there's no harm in this,
At least it don't so appear to me to be amiss.

Now, if any faults in this you find,
Consider them not of the heart, but the mind ;
And remember me as your friend,
One on whom you may always depend ;
Will ever be faithful and true,
Yes, forever, to a friend like you.

WHAT IS HOME WITHOUT A MOTHER?

What is home without a mother?
    Our joys to share, our sorrows to bless ;
For to fill her place there's none other,
    There's no smile nor fond caress,
Like that of a dear patient mother.

What is home without a mother?
    To guide our childish wandering feet,
Whilst tottering along the baby-walks of life,
    Prattling in youthful innocence sweet,
Burdened with no worldly cares nor strife,
    But in infantile purity fondle on mother.

What is home without a mother?
Without her sweet angelic smile,
To drive away our troubles and dull care,
And with sweet comforts bless us all the while,
Traveling life's highway, beset with its many snares,
Though carefully guarded by a fond mother.

What is home without a mother?
Without a happy, cheerful smile to meet us,
As we softly walk in at the open door ;
And with a loving sweet voice to greet us,
As she has so often done before,
With a " God bless you," from mother.

What is home without a mother?
With her hallowed influences to adorn
Our peaceful and happy abodes,
Whilst her prayers, as sweet incense, are borne
For our welfare, as we journey life's uncertain road,
For a final and fairer home with mother.

What is home without a mother?
Our wounds and bruises to heal,
Our headaches and heart-throbs to relieve,
Our faults and failings in her heart conceal,
And with a kind forgiveness tenderly receive
A wayward child back in love to its mother.

What is home without a mother?
O think, erring child, ere 'tis too late,
O think, whilst life's early morn is passing o'er thee,
Yea, think, ere the final decrees of fate
Shall throw its dark shadows before thee,
And rob thy home of a dear mother.

What is home without a mother?
   Seal these precious memories in thy heart,
And ne'er forget, though your days be many to love,
   Those precious words, though you be far apart,
Thy mother a bright seraph in the shining courts above,
   Till then, you can only realize within your heart,
What home is without a mother.

TEMPERANCE BOAT.

O see how the beautiful temperance boat,
On Time's surging billows float;
See, our sails are unfurled and flying,
And to the maddening rage of old demon defying.

Soon this beautiful tranquil bark,
Like a shimmering meteor spark,
Will gently waft us o'er whisky's turbulent sea,
Where bloated faces and blood-shot eyes cease to be.

The temperance cause is gaining ground,
The whisky men are whining around,
"Business interests will be ruined in town."
Then, while we can, this armed foe crush down.

STAR OF HOPE.

All hearts are turned to the radiant star, Hope;
   We hail thee in thy bright form,
We see thy spark at a distance remote,
   Beaming to us in life's fearful storm.

PAST, PRESENT AND FUTURE.

The past, present and future,
  Has marked in its time all nations,
  All ages, and all earth's generations,
The present only is all we can nurture.

The past on eagle wings has flown
  To other realms, far away,
  And the present now we enjoy to-day,
And to-morrow, oh! where? 'twill be unknown.

The future, on Time's speeding wings,
  Is coming with ever-sure tidings,
  Perchance it may be pitiless chidings,
For messages of some kind it surely brings.

A VALENTINE.

My love, as this is St. Valentine's merry day,
A fine excuse for reading, writing and play,
So I write; don't let this little bit of a mickle
Insult you, or make you think me fickle.

For it is not so, but the true depths of love
Will, in spite of all the powers above,
Disguise itself to its object of fancy,
And bid defiance to the world's romancy.

But be that as it may, you silly elf,
I want you to keep that to yourself,
And to no one disclose this rude passion,
Neither at home nor 'mid the haunts of fashion.

For I've always had implicit confidence in you,
Though I know not whether you be false or true ;
And this is only the promptings of a heart,
Whose only design is to merely impart

A secret to one, whom I think never knew
That they were loved by one of the few,
Whose immortal love will never die,
But deep in the unfathomed bosom lie.

And for this, I hope, you will not censure me,
As I'm only telling what I think of thee.
And why not I, have the privileged right,
To express thoughts that perchance would blight
A life of tranquil happiness and peace,
If from the mind they were not released ?

But now let me tell you one thing in time,
And that is, if any conceit in this you find,
You need not think the writer a flatterer,
For it is not so, but like the chatterer,
I delight in having some antic fun,
From playing a trick to making a pun.

PRESENT.

The present only is ours,
   'Tis all we can claim ;
Then let us cherish this passing flower,
   Whilst with us it remains.

And learn life's lessons well,
   In early morn whilst we may ;
Ere dusky eve her shadows, who can tell?
   May soon darken our brightest day.

Then let us with eager grasp,
   Seize each moment as they pass,
To accomplish some good in life's great task,
   For mankind of each and every class.

TO SCOTT.

All alone this morning with a little spare time,
I thought to write you a few words before nine,
As at that time our school opens, you well know,
And in the evening closes at exactly four ;
So you see, I'll have to write in haste,
For there'll be no time for me to waste.
I am only going to tell you of a little story,
When a friend, for a practical joke, was in his glory.

But ah ! 'tis useless for me to sit here all the while,
To ponder, to muse, to get something in style
For you, one who cares so very little
For girls and their intrinsical piddles.
Although you're good looking, suffice to say,
I have seen as good looking many a day,
But did not see any more intelligent than you,
And for better, there's but very few.

But I'll tell you now when you were deceived,
By one in whom you might have conceived,
That to you an idle tale they were telling,
To flatter you, that a young lady's heart was swelling
With fond affection for you, one who could not reciprocate
Love's tender emotion, neither soon nor late.
Perhaps there is, but I assure you it is not mine,
For my business now is out of that line.

And as for the simple effusion of love be made cry,
It will only be the parting hand when I come to die.
But once I did cry in the parlor, 'tis true,
In your presence, but not about you.
But 'twas something sacred and sweet, come to mind
Of the past, when friends around me entwined,
Those I feared I should never more see,
But have since learned you believed it was all for thee.

And since that time I fully understand,
That is why you passed through our land,
And did not stop to tell us girls good-by,
You was afraid we would about you cry.
As this was for your friend a very nice joke,
No harm done, nobody's heart broke,
We will kindly forgive and it forget,
As 'tis not worth remembrance nor regret.

THE LARK.

O see the lark, as he rises on the wing,
  Sails aloft in the air, so light and fair ;
The sweetest melodies he doth sing,
  His heart burdened with no sorrow nor care.

O then be like the lark and sparrow,
  Live, while we may, in the sunshine of to-day,
For we know not what 's in the morrow,
  As our joys oft take wings and fly away.

So let us live and work for the present,
  And not all our ore and good deeds in future store,
But to make our friends both happy and pleasant,
  Let us use them every day more and more.

RUMOR.

Unspairing Rumor sends afloat,
   Many illusive unfounded stories,
Disguised in his beautiful colored coat.
   In deception's base mask he glories.
Yea, idle gossip, on speeding wings,
   Rides on every passing gale,
Whilst riding, swiftly brings,
   Forever some vain idle tale.

ST. VALENTINE'S DAY.

St. Valentine's day,
How merry and gay,
The birds in a sweet lay,

Tell their love tale,
As they float on gentle gale,
With joyous hearts on wing they sail,

To find a loved mate,
To share their fate,
Both early and late;

So boys and girls in love,
Will, like the turtle dove,
And falling dews from above,

In melting words their love unfold,
Beautiful as the shining gold,
If 'tis rude, it must be told,

As it is St. Valentine's day,
And who would dare say,
'Twas wrong to write a love lay.

So they with pen and ink,
Tell what they surely think,
In love words, which together they link

They say you are the idol of their heart
Your sweet voice more melody imparts,
Than the softest note of the silver-toned harp

As it gently falls on the ear,
In accents soft, sweet, and clear,
Treasured in the heart a jewel dear.

THE FALSE ONE.

Oh! why did you flatter this heart of mine,
  That loved thee too well to believe
You would seek the affections to win,
  Only to prove false and better feelings deceive;
One who so faithfully promised to be true,
  And have proved so false to me,
Had not your vows been so fondly pledged and few,
  They might have been easily severed and free.

But they were not so lightly made and spoken,
  You gave them with full assurance to me
That they were true, and would ne'er be broken,
  That you would ever faithful and undisguised be,
Which filled my heart with the purest love,
  That knew no bound nor resting place,
But onward would wing its way far above
  Vicious pride, seeking the only true grace,

That should adorn the champion's helmet in war and love,
　And inspire in his bosom the true worth of confidence given,
In sincerity witnessed by the all-ruling powers above,
　Which ought to ever be sacred, not by sundry ties riven:
And you well remember the day when at noon,
　We were seated on the green 'neath the shady oak,
You were flattering me that your thoughts, like the moon,
　Were ever bright, and progressive, free from tyranny's yoke.

But these vows were not only sealed on earth,
　But in heaven, where no deception is known;
And perhaps at eve, when in gleeful mirth,
　Thou wilt sometimes think of the cheerful tone,
That ever joined you in your happiest tune,
　Yet peradventure, you will find some other one,
With whom you may your leisure moments consume.

But, remember I told you, your love was not deep,
　That it was only a boyish, a childish love,
For half of your promises you would not keep;
　But when fancy suggested, to a distant land you'd shove,
Bidding foes and friends a final adieu.
　You would be borne on the broad-bosomed ocean,
Forgetting old friends, forming others anew,
　To dream of me never, but think it was all a notion.

Ah! so true my words of warning have proved,
　For you have been faithless in your vows to me,
And now to a distant land you have removed,
　Thinking there you are unfettered and free.
You now see that I mistook not your disposition,
　For you're disposed to ramble o'er the wide world,
Always ready to start out on some new expedition,
　With your banner to the breezes unfurled.

But give back the heart you have stolen away,
   And let me repine no more o'er lost love,
But free and unbound let me fly from dismay,
   To my forest home, and be the companion of the turtle dove,
Whose sweet voice will ever cheer my frantic brain,
   And her constancy teach me never to give way,
But from mere fancies of vanity always refrain,
   And never disguise, or a friend's faults betray.

Oh! think how cruel you have proved to be,
   For you have stolen my love away,
Saying you soon would restore the gift to me;
   But you have deceived and filled my heart with dismay,
Yes, deceived a better heart than thine own,
   Which can now only seek in vain
To forget thy treachery, and cease to moan,
   For to think of thee gives but pain.

PARTING AND MEETING.

In our friendly parting and social meeting,
Let us always be sincere in our greeting;
As an open enemy we know how to meet,
But a false friend we never know how to greet.
So then always give a fair, free fight
Of things not what they seem, but in sight
Let us always strive to be, what we pretend to be,
If nothing, be nothing, if something, something be,
Never pretend to be something you are not,
For 'twill never add one joy to life's lot.

SILVER LAKE.

___

SCENE I.

[Lady dressed in a blue costume, bedecked with tinsel stars, reclining on a sofa. Enter Lone Star, dressed in full costume, wearing a cap with large star in front, approaching the lady slowly, speaks:]

Oh! beautiful, lovely, sweet Silver Lake,
  Thou loveliest queen of earth's beauties,
Bedecked with myriads of shining stars,   .
  Glistening on thy bosom, calm, peaceful bosom,
Reflecting my never-fading endless rays of light;
  And yet at my presence thou wilt blush,
Oh! why blush thou at the sight of thy companion.

SILVER LAKE:—

Oh! Lone Star, softly falls thy silvery light,
In limpid streams o'er my bosom bright;
Why wonder at the crimson blushes
That o'er my face so rapidly rushes,
As thy golden beams are brilliantly shining,
And loved thoughts are 'round our hearts entwining.

LONE STAR:—

Sweet Silver Lake, upbraid me not,
  If I thy passion thoughtlessly betrayed,
But on thy tranquil bosom blot
  Mine image where thousands are in beauty arrayed.
Speak ye with thy sweet, silver-toned lips,
  And make my heart leap forth in joy,
Forgetting out of sorrow's cup to sip,
  Draughts of care which soon my peace would destroy.

SILVER LAKE:—

Oh! Lone Star, so beautifully bright,
    Had I your bewitching power,
With ease and grace I surely might
    Charm you into love's sweet bower;
For your bright golden beams,
    O'er my gentle bosom of light,
Like a thousand diamonds' sparkling gleams,
    Ever fills fancy's eye with a happy delight.

LONE STAR:—

Oh! sweet Silver Lake, I must confess
    Without flattery, my love for you,
And the true state of anxiety and distress,
    When for rosy morn I must bid you adieu.
As you are my beloved one, the only one
    On whom I so fondly with rapture gaze,
And behold mine image on thy bosom,
    Brightly reflected in thy mirrored wave.

A thousand tiny stars are shining
    On thy bright glowing face,
And with love's golden beams entwining,
    Will illuminates all space.
Oh, my sweet Silver Lake,
    I must bid you adieu to-night,
For my exit I soon will make,
    For the rosy morn of light.

SILVER LAKE:—

Oh! bright and glorious Star,
    I bid you a good-night,
May nought your happiness mar,
    But soon return your brilliant light.

SCENE II.

[Silver Lake appears alone on the stage, walking back and forth.]

SILVER LAKE:—

Oh! the bright starry heavens above,
　Are twinkling with her shining host,
But where, oh! where is my love,
　The Lone Star of whom all beauties boast,
Like some lonely dove cooing;
　I look around, beneath and above,
For my nightly companion has been wooing
　My tender affections and love.

Methinks I see his lovely face
　Rising far o'er yon distant mountain,
His lovely form with bright rays I trace
　The source of his bright fountain.
Oh! Lone Star, where hast thou hid
　Thy bright and brilliant form?
Come, oh! come at my earnest bid,
　And listen to a friend so warm.

Come, oh! come with thy glowing light,
　And cheer this trembling bosom of mine,
Where a thousand beauties bright
　Will glow at thy blazing shrine.
Come, oh! come, dispel these shadowy clouds
　That have veiled thy face of light,
And with mists of darkness my bosom enshrouds
　From thy beautiful rays so bright.

ENTER LONE STAR:—

I come at thy bid, lovely scenes to behold,
　Where sweet angels are hovering

O'er thy gentle bosom in beauties untold,
　I come to greet thee in thy starry covering.

And with my blazing light of affection,
　All I possess I kindly offer thee;
My love, my hand, and sure protection,
　Hoping in its sweet enchantment happier to be.

For thee, I would withdraw from my starry abode
　In the high heavens bright domain,
And with showers of love thee o'erload,
　In bliss with thee evermore to reign,

And would thy sorrows and cares bless,
　And thy sweet affections caress,
And be thy bright, blazing guide,
　O'er life's rough and rugged tide.

Speak ye out of the depths of thy heart,
　Tell of thy lonely retire,
And if thou hast ever, when apart,
　Thought of my bright attire,

If ever in thy loneliness thou didst yearn
　For thy nightly companion's return,
To shed o'er thy bosom his golden beams,
　Where silvery beauty brightly gleams.

SILVER LAKE:—

Oh! Lone Star so beautiful and endearing,
With your presence so bright and cheering,
Could you doubt as a nightly treasure,
That I hail thee as an enchanted pleasure,

Sought you my love nor shall it be in vain,
Come, rest with me, I'll never give thee pain;

For you shall ever be a welcome guest,
And as a budding bouquet adorn my breast.

LONE STAR:—

With glad acceptance sweet Silver Lake,
I'll be a bouquet on thy bosom bright,
And with thee sweetest pleasures partake,
Be a companion of the beauties of light.

I have read of thee in poetry and song,
And wondered where the fairy muse dwelled;
Thy name on the gentle breezes floats along,
And on fancy's prophetic page plainly spelled.

SILVER LAKE:—

Ah! tell me not poet Lone Star,
That you could not divine,
The pensive fairy near nor far,
When thy natures so closely combine.

For 'twas by intuition's golden pen,
That I did first detect your name,
And wondered in what magic den,
You had stolen your bright fame.

'Twas on the broad page of glorious renown,
That in fancy I began to trace,
The beautiful rays of thy golden crown,
Which in splendor now illumes thy face.

Oh! beautiful Lone Star, so bright,
Tell me if in fame's starry host
You first obtained your sparkling gems of light,
Of which all lovers of beauty proudly boast.

LONE STAR:—

Sweet Silver Lake, ask the winged winds
    That fly through the starry regions far,
If they in their airy flight which extends
    O'er heaven's bright domain, spied a star.

For in earth's primeval creation so grand,
    When the morning stars sang together for joy,
Then I came forth as one of the happy band,
    To dwell in fixed harmony without alloy.

Now to you my origin I have told,
    Please from you obscurity fling,
Your mysteries briefly to me unfold,
    And your bright fountain spring.

SILVER LAKE:—

In hope's bright waters I live,
    In contentment's sylvan bower I dwell;
My humble origin I can easily give,
    The estate from which I fell.

I sprang from a bold sparkling fountain,
High on bright fame's huge mountain,
Gently descending in the shades of solitude sweet,
Here have found a sure and safe retreat,

From the envious reptile's spoil,
Calm and peaceful, free from toil,
I lay motionless, my bosom adorned
With the radiant stars of morn;
No cares of vanity my peace to destroy,
But sip from cups of sweet joy.

SCENE III.

[Silver Lake and Lone Star both appear on the stage together. Lone Star addresses Silver Lake first.]

LONE STAR:—

Oh! sweet Silver Lake of hope,
Thy beauties fade at morn's approach ;
Yea, thy beauties fair and bright,
Will soon be veiled by morn's light.

But radiant day-star, bright Aurora,
Shall cheer and comfort thee in thy sorrow,
That genial lamp of day so warm,
Will change the scenes in a varied form.

SILVER LAKE:—

Oh! bright and beautiful Lone Star,
The thoughts of thy departure mar
My happiness, quietude and peace,
For without thee, pleasure doth cease.

'Tis true, the bright king of day,
With a genial and sparkling ray,
May my gloomy thoughts dispel,
But can never your charms quell.

LONE STAR:—

No, we can both but share equal time,
He at day, at night I am thine,
Nor shall I envy him so bright,
But part from thee in bliss to-night.
Though your beautiful bosom of light
Will soon be screened from my sight,
Yet I know in the heart's home of affection,
I hold a sacred place of sure protection.

SILVER LAKE:—

Oh! Lone Star, you are inclined to flatter,
With your praise and love matter;
Perhaps you think impressions are easily made
On a bosom that reflects every shade.

But, Lone Star, you must ever remember,
In a friend true love to engender;
Plain speeches without gay adorning,
Make's heart's home a bright morning.

LONE STAR:—

But, fair guiltless love, you know
That kind words make the heart glow,
And wooing words which your fancy doth please
To call flattery with such grace and ease,

Are like the gentle sweet breezes of morn,
Pure, devoted, gentle, not like the storm
That rules with a giant-like power,
But like bland caressing tones in a gentle shower.

SILVER LAKE:—

Oh! Lone Star, thy words are mild and fair,
Thy form bright and brilliant are;
Thy soothing tones lull me to sleep,
To dream of thy glances bright and sweet.

Oh! may your gay morning of life,
Be free from care and strife;
And life's evening shades dark and drear,
Ever before your blazing shrine disappear.

May you gently and serenely glide,
O'er life's sea dark and wide;

In Hope's barge filled with joy.
No cares thy pleasure to alloy.

But soon you will bid me adieu,
And hide your glorious form from view,
To visit other scenes than these,
Fanned by some gentle genial breeze.

Though in other climes you will find
No warmer friends than you've left behind,
Yet change of scenes oft-times beget,
Sweet pleasures and vain regret.

LONE STAR:—

Though in distant lands wild I roam,
Far from my friends and loved home.
They will ever hold a sacred place
In sweet memory's broad space.

Though I leave you now, dear lovely friend,
Perhaps through many wild deserts to wend,
I'll return to our sweet, peaceful home,
And never, no never, from thee to roam.

But soon shall my bright face be hid,
And brilliant Aurora reign in my stead,
And far from thee, sweet Silver Lake,
I to other regions must take.

But whilst I am with you to-night,
Dear jewel of my heart's delight,
Give me one word of hope ere I start,
Oh! speak, angel, for soon we must part.

So farewell, now we must part,
This hand in thine, the other on my heart;

A kind and loving heart doth swell,
As the fond words doth tell,

When from the heart they fell,
Mournful as the death-knell,
How in memory they dwell,
Secured in the heart's cell.

In plain words 'tis tenderly imprinted,
In the heart deeply indented,
And on the brow firmly stamped,
On the soul steadfastly tramped.

Mine eyes turned toward ambition's golden mount,
Hastily I speed onward to the bright fount;
In my path my parting tracks plainly spell,
The solemn words, " Fair Silver Lake, farewell."

SILVER LAKE:—

Farewell, oh! beautiful bright Lone Star,
Thou wilt roam from me far,
Perhaps in distant lands far away,
Whilst other beauties around thee play.

They will cheer and beguile your hours
Into love's sweet rural bowers,
And lull your senses into a sweet repose,
Of the past, pretty, faded rose.

————

WHEN wandering through life's forests drear,
When its dark shadows about thee appear,
Oh! then trust thy God, he is near,
And will the cries of his people hear.

CRITICISM.

SCENE I.

[Writer seated at a table reading. Critic walking back and forth on front of the stage addressing the audience.]

CRITIC:—

Ah! 'tis a glorious thing for one to be his own king; to be able and wise enough to see the sappy, half-witted fallacy of others; to be king, lord and master of language, art, profession, passion, fancy, love and fashion. Ah! what a pleasure 'tis to be able to ride the high-horse over their silly, hair-brained fabrications, and look down on these would-be somebodies with contempt, and scourge their weak-witted quibbles with haughty high-flown phrases. Ha! poor ignoramuses, they know not what it is to be above toad-leap. They never see to the end of their husky noses, for the many pimply obstacles which obstruct the sight of their common horse-sense. Some of these poor, brainless creatures are silly enough to think themselves poets. Poor creatures, they are as fool-minded as the hoarse, croaking frogs that make a jingling rhyme every time they raise their heads above water, and swell nigh to bursting themselves to make bulky sounds. For instance, I will repeat to you a piece of poetry I read in a newspaper not long since ; perhaps some of you are acquainted with this piece of effusion; no matter, I don't pretend to know who the author is, and care less. It says some boy, but I rather think from the way it reads, 'tis some beardless editor, that wants a wife, and palms the advertisement off on a boy. Well, here it is, we will see if the most of you don't agree with me in my opinion as to who the author is, when they hear it read. He says:—

" He wants to know if she can milk,
And make his bread and butter,

And go to meeting without her silk,
   To make a show and splutter.
He would like to know if it would hurt
   Her hands, to take up stitches,
Or sew the buttons on his shirt,
   Or make a pair of breeches."

Now, that sounds like a boy, don't it? 'Tis simple enough,
'tis true, but not put up in the right style. He wants to know
if it would hurt her hands to take up stitches, or if she can milk,
advertising for a wife.

A capital idea, indeed,
By making inquiries if she can milk,
A practical genius of a rare breed.
I wonder he don't see poetry in all the trees,
And make rhymes like the humming bees.
I imagine, I see him now in poetry chin deep,
In fancy's cradle by rhymes rocked to sleep.

[Writer rises up from the table, steps forward, responds to
Critic in a harsh tone.]

WRITER:—

Sir, your imagination is indeed vain,
In playing on topics which would drain
The last particle of your braggardism wit,
To produce an article of the same fit.

CRITIC:—

To drain the last particle of my wit,
Indeed to produce an article of equal fit,
Why drain the Atlantic's fathomless abyss,
To over-run a marshy stream like this.

For small streams you know
Make the large ones flow,

And at the rising of the tides,
With boldness o'er small ripples rides.

WRITER:—

Ah! what, compare your feeble mind,
   To the broad-bosomed Atlantic,
Whose proud waves swell o'er all mankind;
   Why, man, your brain must be frantic!

'Tis true, small streams make large ones flow,
   And if I mistake not, you are but a small stream
Running a swift channel far below
   Those on whom you prefer to vent your spleen.

CRITIC:—

My feeble mind, how dare you speak thus
Of a superior, who wouldn't stop to fuss
Over greatness for the sake of a name,
Nor flatter yourself crowned with fame,
For I assure you I am a genius and you are none,
I will test the matter before we are done.

WRITER:—

Ah! my superior, who would doubt the case,
When 'tis so plainly printed on your face,
In letters of enormous size, saying,
Estimated very wise in his own weighing,
You who would not stoop to fuss over a name,
No, for in stooping you would hide but your own shame.

One who boasts over his rank,
Had better keep near his own bank,
And you say I need not myself flatter,
If I did, it would be no matter,
For empty heads, like empty gourds,
For trash and flattery plenty room affords.

7

Ha! my, you are a genius, a queer one.
If I did not know your buzzing hum,
I would sooner think you a "scare-crow,
Eloped from some corn row."
And you say my genius you will test,
Sir, you are quite welcome to do your best.

CRITIC:—

Fie! do my best, with much ease
I can soon cure you of your poetic disease.
You'd sooner think me some scare-crow,
Pray, from what fount did you flow?

WRITER:—

Ah! talk about curing a disease of which
You are inflicted to the highest pitch,
But of a much lower grade than mine,
For 'tis only silly, brainless rhyme.

And, sir, if you are very anxious to know
The fount from which I flow,
'Tis one for which you long have been striving,
But never able to reach with all your contriving.

CRITIC:—

Why, your words are as the thunders pealing,
That make wounds, for which there's no healing.
Now, there's no use for such folly as this,
'Tis a practice and habit you possess my angry Miss.

WRITER:—

Sir, you are no judge of genius, but small matters,
Of silly words and ragged tatters ;
And if my words wound you so deep,
Out of their reach you had better keep.

CRITIC:—

 Ah! there's no use in talking to you,
 For I plainly see nothing will do,
 But I must give in to your selfish will,
 Though wrong, you'll have your way still.

 Yes, for my way is always the right way,
 And there's no sense in anything you say,
 For right is right, and will no one wrong,
 So that is the short of it and long.

SCENE II.

[Writer seated at a table reading, rises slowly and walks to the front of stage addresses the audience.]

WRITER:—

 What a world is this. Never-tiring improvement ceases not to roll her great and mighty wheel of reformation through the endless ages, refining man, polishing nature, and ultimately makes a completion of the great combined works of Deity. See here [holding up some books] are samples of intellect. The intellect of a few great writers of the day, and of some who have forever past away. Their physical bodies have long lain 'neath the sod, yet their minds of intellect still live in the memory, crowned with fresh laurels gathered from bright fame's flowery wreath. Their lives were as the wild dashing sea, smoothly gliding on through the " sequestered vales" of peace, then again beset with the stormy clouds of sorrow.

  And though their lives like autumn storm,
  To us is forever past and gone,
  Yet their foot-prints are distinctly plain,
  On Time's sea-shore, though there long have lain.

 Theirs is an immortal name, written on every passing breeze, perfumed by every lovely flower, sung by every sweet songster and hailed with that bright meteor, the glorious king of day, shedding his brilliant lustre at the shrine of wisdom. Oh! that we might live as— [Enter Critic.]

Ah! a good morning and health to thee, Madam Villittie. I am sure you are looking pensive this morning. Prithee, good lady, what may be the cause of thy melancholy ; 'tis not some sad story you've been reading that has caused this dreadful reverie. Ah! 'tis of fallen greatness, I suppose, for here I see [picking up a book] some of your favorite authors, some of the greatest productions that have ever been put forth. Ah! perhaps I am intruding. [Starts off. Writer turns and speaks.]

Not at all, Sir Voleka. I had been perusing some of my favorite authors, and was in deep meditation, thinking what giant minds they must have possessed, and was speaking of their greatness as you came in. Please to be seated [hands a chair], Sir Voleka, and excuse the reception you met with from your friend.

CRITIC:—

Most assuredly, Madam Villittie, I will excuse you, as you were alone meditating this bright beautiful morning, and musing over some old works of your favorite authors. Allow me, Madam Villittie, to beg your pardon for being before time, as I have been very anxious to see you since our conversible interview on last evening about matters of no small importance. I heartily beg your pardon for being so hasty in my remarks, as well as in my sarcastic insinuations.

WRITER:—

I grant your pardon with great pleasure, Sir Voleka, and hope we shall have a fine time this morning. Here are some poetical works on the table [picks up a book] with which I think we can amuse ourselves. Here is a "Lover's Poem." What do you think, the author of this article confined himself to his room three days and nights to write a verse on that great passion called Love.   Listen to what he says:—   [Reads a verse.]

> Love, 'tis a killing thing,
> It flits from wing to wing ;
> And as sure as I am in my boots,
> It tears oak trees up by the roots.

CRITIC:—

Ah! indeed a poet ; yes, a Byron, unlike what the world ever saw ; without a parallel, none but himself could be his parallel.

WRITER:—

Here is [turns a leaf] another piece, let me read it to you, and hear your opinion of it.

CRITIC:—

Well, read it, but if it is like the other, it won't be worth an opinion.

WRITER:—

It will be a poor thing, indeed, if it is not worth your opinion.

CRITIC:—

What, do you mean to insult me?

WRITER:—

Not at all, Sir Voleka, if you won't be insulted at the truth.

CRITIC:—

At the truth?   I presume you estimate my opinion worth nothing, and prove your estimation by saying 'tis the truth.

WRITER:—

Not at all, Sir Voleka, for 'tis plain enough without proof ; what the world can see needs no proof.

CRITIC:—

Ah! Madam Villittie, I see you love to quarrel, and that is what you are after ; but I don't intend quarrelling with you, for I consider it but a weakness.

WRITER:—

And we are the weaker vessel, I suppose. Well, I'll read
the piece, and we'll be in good humor. It is a lady writing, she
says:—

> " I went into the garden to get 'taters,
> And walked in my fine gaiters,
> Thinking of nothing but my beau,
> As all foolish girls do, you know.

> " And the first thing I knew,
> I run over a stump and tore my shoe,
> Forgetting as sure as I'm a sinner,
> What I went to get for dinner.

> " For instead of getting 'taters,
> I got a pan of termaters,
> And in a big hurry to get back,
> I spilt 'em all, falling in my track.
> My sweetheart seeing me fall,
> In a sweet undertone did bawl.

> " ' Oh! sweet love did it hurt thee,'
> And picking me up, kissed me,
> Saying, " My sweet turtle-dove,
> 'Tis you I dearly love.

> " ' O say you'll be my wife,
> All your long life ;
> For without you I can't be happy,
> For about you my head is most sappy.'

> " I looked up in his lovely face,
> And thinking of his lonely case,
> And with a sweet heavenly smile,
> Him kissing me all the while,

"Answered that dear word, 'Yes,
If my Dad will buy me a dress.'
I'll tell you no more of the rest,
But you may be sure we were blest."

CRITIC:—

Ha! the accident proved quite a lucky thing for her. Well, as you have asked my opinion on this piece, I will just say she was very lucky in this instance, though sometimes such luck proves very unfortunate in the end. It is a fine composition, the subject a very delicate one, and was handled finely. She certainly must have gone off in a love trance, and visited that dreamy land where all the girls go to in our section to make forked matches, and prime them with the friction of love, to touch off the mighty cannon which slays all the honeyed boys that are strung on the knotty string of matrimony. Let me see the book. [Takes it, and turns a leaf.] Why, here is something [reads], "A Boy's Courtship," listen to what he says, and let me have your opinion, as you have had mine for some time.

WRITER:—

You shall have it, Sir Voleka, with pleasure.

CRITIC:—

Well, here it is. He says:—

"I went out a courting one day,
All very fine and gay;
I had to ride but three miles,
Until I reached her honey smiles;
My steed traveled at a pretty rate,
Soon he landed me at the gate.

"And there sat my darling in full dress,
I caught her round the neck, to press
Her ruby lips, so sweet, to mine.
She gave me a loving sign;

I sighed, and leisurely leaned back,
Our lips going smicky smack.

"And her papa, just about that time,
Slowly stepped up from behind,
Said, 'Wretch, ungrateful daughter,
Bring your papa some cool water.'
I tried hard to raise a conversation,
When the toe of his boot said, 'Emancipation.'

"I tried with him the case to reason,
But the old man said it was out of all season.
So then what do you reckon I did,
Why, right over the fence, without a shirt, I slid,
Falling into a large box of mortar,
Forgetting the old man's lovely daughter.

"I piteously cried for some one to help,
And the first thing I felt,
Was the old man's leather strap,
Over my head going spat, spat,
I scrambling up to the old man said,
'O, pray, have mercy on this silly head,

"'For if ever I get out of this bad scrape,
I never will another such a trip make.'
He, looking angrily to me, said,
'No, you can never my daughter wed,
And the sooner you my premises leave,
For the less you will have to grieve.'

"So, raising my hat with a low bow,
I bid him good morning, as well as I knew how.
So that fatal but lucky blunder,
Cut my love for girls asunder ;

And an old bachelor I have lived to be,
And the faults of boyhood days plainly see."

How do you like this?

WRITER:—

Well, I really do admire his civility, as well as the courtesy, he showed to the exasperated old man that gave him such a cool welcome and hearty good-by.

CRITIC:—

It was most too much of a hearty good-bye; you had better said hardy, instead of hearty, it would have been more appropriate.

WRITER:—

That would only be your opinion of it.

CRITIC:—

My opinion I think would be correct.

WRITER:—

Yes, I presume you are very wise in your own estimation; you always think your opinions are correct.

CRITIC:—

Well, madam, I allow you the same privilege.

WRITER:—

Only because you can't help yourself.

CRITIC:—

If I could, it would be all the same, for if you think nothing of yourself, nobody else will.

WRITER:—

'Tis true, but others seldom over-rate your value as you do yourself sometimes.

CRITIC:—

I think that rather a broad assertion to make to a friend.

WRITER:—

But nevertheless true.

CRITIC:—

Well, Madam Villittie, I see there's no use in my trying to get along with you, for 'tis impossible, unless I agree in every-thing you say.

WRITER:—

Sir, if you don't see proper to get along with me, you can get along without me.

CRITIC:—

You misconstrue everything I say or mean.

WRITER:—

I always mean just what I say, and say just what I mean.

CRITIC:—

Yes, but other people, perhaps, are not so charitable as yourself; do not as you do every time.

WRITER:—

I never bargained to be responsible for other people's actions, and wouldn't have them to do as I do every time, for then I know we would always be at variance.

CRITIC:—

Well let's not get mad at each other. I thought you said this morning we would have a fine time.

WRITER:—

I said, I hoped we would have a fine time, and we will, if you'll only be agreeable, for I am sure I am fond of fine times and fine things too.

CRITIC:—

Well, if you are, let us have another piece on the strength of it. [Turns a leaf.] Let me see, I want to find something laugh-able this time; perhaps if I can have you indulge in a hearty laugh, then you'll be in a good humor with me and the world beside. [Turns another leaf.] Well, here it is, the very piece itself. 'Tis the sentiments of a devoted lover to his adored Miss. Now hear what he says on the all-inspiring passion called Love·

I know you will admire his eloquence. [Reads aloud,] " Lines to Miss Polly Ann Higgins."

" Oh! my dear sweet Polly Ann,
When over this world I scan,
There is none I can find,
So pretty and kind,   ·
As my dear sweet Polly Ann,
In all this sunny land.

" Though the storms around me roar,
And thunders sound ten-score,
Can never drown my love
For thee, my sweet darling dove ;
And o'er the highest mountains I'd jump,
For thee, my sweet golden lump.

" And thou art as precious to my eye,
As the most brilliant dye,
For thou art a sweet little flower,
Blooming in my heart's love bower ;
And oh! thy red rosy lips to meet
In a love-kiss, 'tis so charming sweet.

" And when I fold my arms around you,
I think I have bound you
Close to the heart you adore,
And one you love a score.
Ah! no tongue can ever tell,
The depth you lie in the heart's deep well."

CRITIC:—
    Isn't it charming, lovely, and sweet?

WRITER:—
    Delightful ; to be sure he has some good ideas, if they were well expressed.

CRITIC:—

So he has; but not expressing them right is the great mistake of a good many others. A good idea well expressed is a beautiful thing, and seldom found; but like the precious pearls of the deep, if too plentiful, they become common and cease to be prized.

WRITER:—

Ha! your philosophy finely coincides with that of a lady who went into a dry goods house to purchase a fashionable dress. When the merchant threw her down one, she exclaimed, "Ah! that's too common, everybody's got a dress like that. I want something new and odd." Now, you see, she wanted to be fashionable, yet she wanted something like nobody else.

CRITIC:—

It does not require unison and uniformity to be fashionable. You may see a great many ladies and gentlemen dressed fashionable, yet not alike, something little different.

WRITER:—

I think we have rather a mixed metaphor, fashion and value. Anything may be common and fashionable, yet valueless. If the golden pearls of the mighty deep, like the numerous leaves of the wild old forest, were scattered all over this wide globe, they would yet be valuable.

CRITIC:—

Well, that let's me out.

SCENE III.

[Writer seated at a table writing, when Critic enters, and speaks:]

A good evening to the Madam Villittic. I have more to inquire about. I find here [picks up a book from the table] in these works on the table many unmarked quotations. Why is this? It surely was not the intention of the author to steal from other writers, and it could not be done through ignorance; and now I should like very much to know something about this matter.

WRITER:—

Sir Voleka, I fear you have called on a very weak intelligencer for the desired information. Had I your pretended ability I should have called on a better commentator than myself.

CRITIC:—

Madame Villittie, you don't seem to have an exalted opinion of yourself.

WRITER:—

Not at all, Sir Voleka, my opinions never run ahead of my better judgment.

CRITIC:—

Well, that's very good, Madam Villittie. You always seem to be very considerate in your decision.

WRITER:—

Sir, I think we should always be judicious in placing an estimate on the value of other writers' productions, for, if like ourselves, they are not perfection.

CRITIC:—

That's so, Madam Villittie, not perfection. That word perfection is a rare blossom, and seldom blooms this side of heaven.

WRITER:—

Well, to proceed, what information is wanted.

CRITIC:—

I want to know why it is that I see in the works of two or three different authors the same phrases used, and no marked quotations. I always thought when I used the words of another, it was right to show where I got them. I had as soon be caught stealing a sheep as stealing a piece of poetry.

WRITER:—

Yes, for theft can't be anything else than theft, clothe it as you will; but I don't suppose they meant to steal it, but their ideas being nearly the same, expressed them alike. For instance, you and I might, whilst viewing the last amber rays of the sinking sun, write a piece of poetry entitled, "The Golden Sunset." Now, who would have to use it as a quotation? You would claim it as your original thought or idea, and I would think it my own, and rightfully it would belong to us both.

CRITIC:—

Madam Villittie, your discrimination is clearly drawn from the fountain-head of perfection, for I see clearly, since you have so finely and discreetly illustrated it, that every word we speak might be termed a quotation, if quoted, because it had been used by another, for there is not a word in the English language but what has been used long before our day. Madam Villittie I am under many obligations to you for this explanation, and feel happily gratified at your beneficent disposition toward the feelings of others.

WRITER:—

Sir Voleka you are quite welcome to all the good I have done you.

CRITIC:—

Madam Villittie, I do indeed feel amply compensated for my evening's call, and assure you the treasures you have disclosed to me this evening will be carefully stored away among the many valuables of my heart.

WRITER:—

Sir Voleka, I fear you are a soft-soaper. Think not I am a mystified dupe to be caught in your box-trap flattery.

CRITIC:—

Madam Villittie, I am indeed sorry that you have such an opinion of a friend who would sacrifice every pleasure for your comfort and happinesss.

WRITER:—

Yes, you would sacrifice pleasure in one way, I have no doubt, and that would be the pleasure the wolf would have in order to catch the lamb.

CRITIC:—

Ah! Madam Villittie, think me not deceitful. I avow you are from the very door of perfection, and have passed through the flowery garden of scholarship and reaped an adequate store of knowledge.

WRITER:—

Now begin with your insipid routine of preposterous blan diloquence to curry favor with my good opinion.

CRITIC:—

With your good opinion, Madam Villittie; yes, your good opinion; you have no good opinion of me, I am sure. You would be angry with me no matter what I would say or do.

WRITER:—

Yes, because you are always saying or doing something you ought not.

CRITIC:—

Well, what must I say? Tell me something to say that you wont get mad at.

WRITER:—

You had better say nothing at all than to say what you do sometimes, as it would be much pleasanter to us both, I assure you, for there is not anything I hate worse than silly cajolery. You couldn't insult my dignity sooner.

CRITIC:—

Your dignity, to be sure; your dignity is easily insulted. I fear you'd most dance a tune set to music by an innocent flea, who only meant to draw a little sweet essence from thy enchanting form.

WRITER:—

I don't know whose dignity wouldn't be insulted by such a brainless creature as you are. Your brazen looks are sufficient to insult the dignity of an honest dog.

CRITIC:—

Well, Madam Villittie, I can say one thing which I think would become you very much, and that is for you not to be so petulant about small matters; you are so waspish, an angel couldn't get along with you.

WRITER:—

Not such an angel as you are.

CRITIC:—

Now, come out of all this, and we can get along perhaps at a distance that we can't scarcely hear each other at the highest key.

WRITER:—

Sir Voleka, your taste and mine widely differ. What you think would become me, other people would abhor. Do you suppose for a moment, if I am the weaker vessel, that I would like a ninny-hammer gulp down your silly flattery, and fatten on it like a pig on potatoes ; and, Sir Voleka, you have but a weak idea of small matters, if you call the insignificant prattle you have been using at my expense, a small matter; and you say I am so waspish, you may thank your stars that I am not a wasp, if I were, I would soon sting you out of your vegetable kingdom.

CRITIC:—

Yes, that you would do, I admit, and believing you are one, I shall soon leave this unwholesome abode of one of the most petulant beings on earth, who stoops to low things, undermining reason, ruining herself in all her blooming youth, stinging herself to the heart's core, causing her to flee to the desert land of nothingness. So now I will be—be— [starts off and looks back] I fear you will follow me. [Writer runs after him with a broom-stick, and speaks as he goes out:]

Go, you white-washer, toad-eater, touter-spaniel, claw-back, flunkey, lick-spittle, pick-thank, ear-wig, doer of dirty work, sir.

ACROSTICS.

D ay-dreams of happiness and golden sunshine,
E ver on the fleeting wings of endless time,
L ay their ample robes so beautifully fair,
I n lovely garlands so rich and rare,
L earning us in silence life's ills to bear,
A s gently falls the silvery frosts of age,
H arbingers of peace to the time-worn sage.

A s the life-boat quietly and smoothly glides,
N ewly borne o'er life's sea by the heaving tides,
N ow safely anchored on the further shore.

M elodies soft and low greet thee evermore,
E nter in with the loved ones of yore,
L eave behind earthly cares, for they come no more,
T o trouble our hearts nor tear-stain our brow,
O nce safely landed over the river, I trow
N o evil tidings can ever come to us now.

H ark! hear your mother's gentle voice, ·
E ver in her tender love gladly rejoice,
L isten to her softest tones sweetly spoken,
E nliven her dull hours by some kind token,
N ever let your affection for her be broken.

I n your bright days of happy sunshine,
D eny thyself idle pleasures in saving thy time,
A cquiring the precious pearls from wisdom's mine.

9

M ay you always through life ever remember,
A ffection for thy mother, respectful and tender,
G oes with God's blessings promised to you,
G iven as a moral obligation for every one to do,
I n life's ever-fluctuating scenes continually rising,.
E mbalms our happy days, quells our surmisings.

———

A dmire not fools, because of their fine dress,
D evoid of principle, they try to impress
E rror in the minds of the unsuspecting youth.
L isten not to their fabrications of untruth,
L est they in an unguarded moment of time,
E nter in and sow the seeds of crime.

———

M any false glories shed their lambent light,
E ver in the pathway of childhood so bright,
L eave not the beaten paths thy friends have trod,.
T urn not to either side but onward plod,
O nly take the old land-mark for your guide,
N icely o'er life's surging sea you will safely ride.

———

L oiter not in the dark paths of sin,
I n haste flee from its strong power,
Z ealous of the good from others you may win.
Z ephyrs of love, must like a sweet flower,
I n your life shed affection's sweet perfume,
E ver at eventide's hour will your path illume..

———

E ver remember that life's shadows fall,
L ate in the afternoon of years ;
L et precious truth like a strong wall,
A round you guard your fears.

S teep, steep, higher, higher,
A las! alas! hopes have fled,
L ike snow before the fire,
L eaving both disaster and dread,
I n loneliness ever to retire,
E vermore to slumber with the dead.

———

M any bright and happy hopes lie before thee,
A childhood's joys are passing o'er thee,
U nfolding the sweet pleasures of youthful life,
D riving away dull care and bitter strife.

———

J oin the cold water army now,
E ver to its clear crystal shrine bow,
S ee our sails are hoisted and flying,
S oon our bark safely in harbor will be lying,
I nscribed on our banner, "Never Falter,"
E ver, ever drink, clear sparkling water.

———

H owbeit, spare no pains in search of truth,
U nless you store the mind well in youth.
T ake care that the seeds of folly and sin,
T arnish not thy pure youthful soul within.
O ft you may have in life's declining years,
N eglect of duty meet you in blinding tears.

———

K ind deeds, kind words, can never die,
E ven though in the humblest walks they lie,
L ike the shining stars in the heavens bright,
L ight up the mid-darkness of the night.
E ver cheer the dreary path-way of life,
Y ears of pleasure but days of strife.

H eaven's glories beam fair and bright,
A fter the gloomy darkness of dreary night
R ustles away on her airy wings of light.
V isions fair are seen most everywhere,
E ver changing their forms so beautifully fair,
Y ielding up their beauties so rich and rare.

———

F leeting, childish joys,
R apidly on Time's speeding wings,
A lways sweetest pleasure brings.
N ature, when her juvenile glee sings,
C heerily with wee girls and boys,
I n their happiest songs of love,
S hedding sunlight from above.

———

L et thy days of happy, innocent youth,
U nder the impression of beautiful truth,
L end to your charms an air of grace,
U nlike other treasures, with smiles wreathe thy face.

———

J ustify no evil-doer,
O n his shrewd acts ;
H owever, he be a wooer,
N ote only true facts.

———

C ould you look o'er life's troubled sea,
H ow the surging billows rise in majesty,
I n swelling waves of ever changing light,
L istless on the shores of eternal night.
D ays of innocence well spent in youth,
E ver like the bright gems of truth,
W ill the sorrows of life gently soothe.

M y love for thee is pure,
A nd ask yours to make it secure ;
R adiant stars around thee shine,
Y ou are an angel bewitching my mind.

J ocund thy voice be on the breeze,
U nmolested thy peace and happiness be,
L ike gypsies before thee, lovers are on their knees,
I n constant fear they give you their pleas,
A ll their pleadings are alas! but vain.

N ear the crystal stream of life,
E ver through dangers dark and rife,
L isten to the fairy boatman's oar,
L end an ear to the music on the shore,
I n life's pilgrimage sorrowing here,
E ver look to our God, for he is near.

M ay you gently and serenely glide,
O 'er life's sea dark and wide,
L anding safely on the evergreen shore,
L istening to the beautiful songs of the evermore;
I n shining robes of purest white,
E ver be an angel of eternal light.

M orning star, 'tis thee,
A ll hail! thou queen of stars.
"R oll on thou deep blue sea,"
'T is the pride of shining stars ;
H ow welcome a guide for the free,
A ll hail thee, thou queen of stars.

J oy and gladness will with life's pleasures,
E ver be cherished as our richest treasures;
S o let us, whilst life's weary road we travel,
S oothe its sorrows, its troubles unravel,
I n the happy thoughts of childish glee,
E ver live in the sunshine of life so free.

———

J udge ye not the person by their dress,
E steem them for the noble qualities they possess,
N ever the gee-gaws of a cox-comb admire,
N ever his fair-spoken blandiloquence desire;
I n self-respect civil gentility always demand,
E nhance thy charms only by virtue's command.

———

M orning star of the day,
I hail thee, thou art man's guide.
L eave me not without one ray,
D ecuple brighter than great Jupiter's pride, ı
R eceive me into thy orbit ray,
E re life's tide wafts me o'er death's dark sea,
D eath is no terror in the sight of thee.

SENIOR DEPARTMENT.

DEPARTED FRIENDS.

Oft do I think of dear departed friends,
When I hear the low murmuring winds
That in sweet melody around me are sighing,
And the moaning of withered leaves underneath them lying,
Sounding their last requiem in a mournful strain,
Teaching us that all idle pleasures are vain.

And oft doth my mind wander back to memory dear,
When many dangers in life's merry morn we had to fear.
But onward, onward, we are speeding through life,
And may expect to meet with care and strife;
Let us be content with our humble station,
And seek a place above where there is no temptation.

The boundless ocean, her gigantic waves roll
In deep majesty o'er many a precious soul,
Whose lives were spent toiling a fortune to save.
But alas! in their striving they found a watery grave,
Where music is made by the shrieking winds,
A mournful dirge to their distressed friends.

But from this vale of tears they have passed away,
To brighter realms where reigns endless day;
And their untimely fate let us not deplore,
For our grief can never their lives restore,
But in adversity let us be resigned to our Master's will,
And all his commandments try to fulfill.

MAN.

Man is but a shadow, a bright vision,
   Riding on the stormy wings of time,
To the land of chaos, or the fair elysian,
   Where the many sweet anthems chime.

Man is but a taper, a florid light,
   Glistening on Time's golden page,
Shining but a moment, vanishing out of sight,
   To the antiquated palace of hoary age.

Man is but a spark, a glaring flame,
   Blazing on Time's shadowy landscape.
Fades away, and nought but the name,
   Survives the final escape.

Man is but a phantom, a frightful ghost,
   Walking o'er Time's ruthless sword,
To be cut down like the multitudinous host,
   Which to other climes have forever soared.

Man is but a vapor, an imaginary dream,
   Floating swiftly on Time's endless wings,
Swallowed up in Death's cyclopean stream,
   Lamenting in woe, or in happiness sings.

THE VALEDICTORY.

Adieu to the Sunny South, our loved home,
"The land of the noble and free;"
Our fondest farewell we breathe to thee,
May kind heaven bless thee, though far away we roam.

Yes, far, far away we soon will be borne,
On the great waters of the deep,
And by muttering winds be lulled to sleep,
To dream of loved ones from whom we are rudely torn.

Yes, ruthlessly torn from home and friends,
To sojourn in a land far away,
'Mid strangers, none to welcome our stay,
Save the warbling songster and soft-sighing winds,

Which seems to breathe into our benighted souls,
Something sacred and sweet,
To cheer us, whilst on the retreat,
Inspiring a hope within our mind consoles.

And now to our friends we bid a kind farewell,
May they our sorrows never know,
But the mercies of a kind providence on them bestow
The richest blessings, and their fears for our safety quell.

RACE OF MAN.

The races of men, wonderfully have been
Spread all o'er this globe, in varieties of robe,
From the north polar star, to sunny regions far,
From the old eastern land, to the gold western strand.

From the sunny fountains, to the snowy mountains,
From the genial breezes, to the cold icy freezes,
The races of men, wonderfully have been,
Scattered far and near, through forests wild and drear.

The races of men, wonderfully have been
Many colors made, both white, black, and a lighter shade.
Through woods wild they roam, seeking some new home,
Where in woodland bowers, grow the fairest flowers.

The races of men, wonderfully have been
Made in many kinds, and divided in many minds.
Some have been made, through sorrow's vale to wade,
Whilst others in elysian bowers, spend many happy hours.

Some to dream of fountains bright, and sparkling gems of light,
With the brilliant gems of morn, their bosoms to adorn.
Some made to dream, of bright golden stream,
"Where 'mid its cool waters lave," many sons of the brave.

THE SOUL A MIRROR.

The soul 's a mirror of beauty refined,
It speaks, it lives within the mind,
And is the vital spark of human life,
Without it there would be neither joy nor strife,
But human existence would prove an empty space,
Filled with animals of quite a different race.

Yes, the soul 's a mirror of beauty divine,
In it all the beauties of nature combine,
From the most exalted to the humblest door,
Among the proud, the rich, and poor,
Are alike possessed of the same great prize,
It dwells with the ignorant as well as the wise.

The soul 's a mirror of beauty that shines
Within man, and around him entwines
True friendship, imprinted in letters of gold,
On the face of the enlightened soul,
Which will ne'er be erased by Time's fingers,
But in eternity their lines still brighter lingers.

The soul 's a mirror, reflecting in every age,
The noble thoughts of Deity on Life's golden page,
Engraven by the great Author of all divine,
The generous impulse within the opening mind,
Born to live in eternity's heavenly bliss,
Or in regions of woe, the fathomless abyss.

FUTURE.

We anxiously await the future, to bring
    Some sweet tidings of joy;
It hastily comes, but no tidings bring,
    Only the death trumpet proclaims man to destroy.

Oh! the cheering hope of the future,
    How pleasant the scenes of the morrow;
Still hoping, the present we nurture,
    From the past we cannot borrow.

We live in hope of future life,
    To be a pleasant road to travel;
But alas! when it comes 'tis all strife,
    For time will all things unravel.

Time is as the life of man,
    That flourisheth and fadeth evermore;
'Tis all, all governed by one mighty hand,
    It is that Father who rules now and evermore.

THE FARMER.

The farmer in his merry song,
With his whip in hand, trudges along,
As if his life was an anthem of joy,
Doth his hands and mind employ.

He labors his wealth to promote,
Either whistling a tune or humming a note;
He asks not fame nor wealth,
His hard labor is only good for health.

He loves work, for 'tis happy employment,
To have plenty of funds for future enjoyment.
In the day he labors, at night he rests
In calm repose, not haunted by midnight pests.

In spring he rejoices to see,
The storms over and leaves on the tree.
'Then with a merry voice he sings,
"It is planting time," and the grain he flings.

In the morning he rises with the lark,
And off to his work as quick as a spark;
"This day," with a jolly voice he cries,
"Shall count one," then to his labor he flies.

And in summer, when tilling is o'er,
His grain to reap, his fruit to store,
He reaps with a machine of superior kind,
That gathers it up in sheaves to bind.

In autumn he gathers fruit of various kinds,
For he knows how himself best to suit.
Nevertheless puzzling his mind,
Over a mass of grapes for a barrel of wine.

When winter comes, with his forage in the barn,
More employment yet, but not on the farm;
It is the care of the farm stock and his steed,
That is so faithful and indispensable in need.

The farmer's life is a world of joy,
He doth his body and mind employ,
In preparing for future happiness,
Who never knows scant want's distress.

With the farmer, peace and contentment dwell,
He has no rugged waves of trouble to quell,
No thirst of ambitious power to haunt his mind,
Of all others he is the happiest of mankind.

LIFE.

What is life?
'Tis but a fitful dream
Of fancy, that teem
With dangers rife.

The many sports
In life that allures us on,
Are no sooner realized than gone,
To other courts.

What is life?
'Tis a scene of joy and woes,
Continually rising as our foes,
To terminate strife.

To live aright,
O let us strive with unceasing care,
So that we may join worlds more fair,
Filled with delight.

With supreme joy,
We may live with our Maker there,
Where reigneth neither sorrow nor care,
Only blissful joy.

WOMAN'S RIGHTS.

Woman's rights, they say, are in the house,
  Around the fireside snugly sitting.
But who are they? the men of course,
  Who spend their time in chewing and spitting.

Woman's rights, ah! dear me, what a tale
  To go forth, that a woman has any rights,
Save to milk the cow, and clean the pail,
  Sweep the floors, and make the lights.

Woman's rights, what are they, pray do tell?
  Is it not to wash, to cook, and to brush,
To baste, to seam, to stitch, and to fell,
  As well as the baby's cries to hush?

Woman's rights, they say, what does it mean?
  Can it be a higher or a nobler life,
Where earth's pleasures will more surely beam,
  Than to be called a man's dear darling wife?

Woman's rights, to be sure, have they none?
  O, yes, the world over will agree,
That woman over man the greatest victory won,
  When she induced him to eat of the forbidden tree.

Woman's rights, we must surely confess,
  Begin to assume matters of great import.

Grant her rights and her wrongs redress,
　　Then she will anchor safely in her peerless port.

Woman's rights, and why not adjust their claim,
　　Since God in his wisdom made them free?
Should man in his weakness boast in vain,
　　His authority to rule or her superior be?

Woman's rights you may laugh to scorn,
　　Yet in your proud vauntings can never
Quell the untiring spirit which in woman is born,
　　To shine as the stars in heaven forever.

Woman's rights, no doubt, seems to vex
　　The princely lords and ladies of our land,
Who in their highness try to stigmatize our sex,
　　And our cries for liberty with shame to brand.

Woman's rights, perhaps the favored few,
　　Who with life's rarest luxuries abound,
Do not so keenly feel need like I and you,
　　Who have not the necessaries of life found.

Woman's rights, I dare say, ere long,
　　Will be recognized throughout the land,
As an unfettered sceptre of right and not wrong,
　　When honest labor will respect command.

Woman's rights, now the query is, what are they?
　　Is it not to think and act for herself alone,
As she is responsible, not others, for the way
　　She lives a life of her own.

Woman's rights, why not claim their due,
　　As the world's renown on them depend?
Are not their acts among the noble and true,
　　As through the rugged ways of life they wend?

Woman's rights, why not merit the same
  As lordly man, who in his mind,
Regards himself the world's rock and brain,
  The woman the clay and the sand.

BE MINDFUL OF DEATH.

Oh! let us ever be mindful of death,
  For he lurks in every flower,
  Bending them to his power,
Withering all nature in his burning breath.

He steals with a noiseless tread 'mid the throng,
  Culling the fairest flowers,
  From our earthly bowers,
To shrink within in his iron grasp so strong.

Oh! Death, what a cruel monster thou art,
  Robbing us of our friends so dear,
  Blinding our eyes with many a tear,
Piercing our happiness with thy keen darts.

THE REBEL.

The rebel, far from the land of his nativity,
  To the sunny shores of the South has fled,
There to earn his living by hard activity,
  And the wayfarer's path to tread.

Robbed of home, friends, and all that is dear,
  He seeks a land, wild, trackless, and unknown;
Breathes a long farewell, and drops a tear,
  For the land of his birth and loved home.

Away, far away, in distant lands he roams,
  Wearied of the joys transient as the dew,
Which so soon vanishes from life's morn,
  And forever fades from his view.

And oh! how oft he casts a long lingering look,
  Back on memory's antique page,
When in youthful life, perhaps by some little nook,
  Was planning an honorable old age.

But alas! little did he then dream of the woe,
  That should so soon betide him,
And his loved countrymen become his foe,
  And with cold satire deride him.

Though from home and friends far away,
  His memory will ever be green
In the hearts of those who can never repay,
  The debt of love, though ever so keen.

Yes, long will he live green in fond remembrance,
  For his image is engraven on the hearts
Of the friends, that bear a kindly resemblance
  To the fair flower whose fragrance a balm imparts.

And now a kind farewell to the poor exile,
  May some new resplendent glory
Crown his life, and though he be ten thousand miles,
  May he return to tell the story.

THE PRISONER.

Here in dungeon bars I lay,
  To pine my life out in grief,
O hearken, master, to what I say,
  Give an attentive ear, a word of relief.

9

My sufferings are but pangs of woe,
  Which are a kindling flame,
To lay destruction on my foe,
  Who is only grasping for fame.

Oh! ye villainous blood-hound seekers,
  Who delight in cruel deeds of shame,
To glut your stomachs, your money leekers,
  To bear among your friends a great name.

Ye heedless wretches, for a season of pleasure,
  You would drag down to an early grave,
A widow's son, her only heart's treasure,
  So that you could ride high on honor's wave.

Oh! ye head-long blood-hound villains,
  You will never know till it is too late,
When to cease your infamous killing,
  For soon you may share your victim's fate.

Thy country lies in disgrace and shame,
  Through thy insatiate thirst of blood,
You have shattered the main-mast of your country for name,
  And marked with blood the rank you stood.

THE SOUND OF BATTLE.

Hark! the solemn sound of battle,
  Echoes in forest, opens in plain,
Never cease the cars to rattle
  'Round the banners of the slain,
  Young heroes there sleep ever to remain.

The silent slumber, the long sweet sleep,
　From which none ever wake to weep.
Sleep on, ye honored sons of the brave,
　May naught ever disturb thy quiet graves,
　But sweet flowers of kind friends o'er thee wave

FORSAKEN.

Ah! the thunders are loudly pealing,
　Though their anger I heed not,
But steady I gaze upon the ceiling,
　Quiet with my present lot.

She has forsaken, ah! deserted me,
　Ambition, pride, and fearless heart,
Will ever steadily brace me,
　Even if my path be dark.

'Tis a pity, yet 'tis true,
　My heart's affection did melt,
When first I loved you,
　And in your presence dwelt.

Oh! ye gods of the earth,
　Where is my resting place?
Is there no joyful mirth,
　To change this sullied face?

Yes, there is glory, honor, and fame,
　Lying in heaps as it were gold;
'Tis my great and glorious name,
　Its elastic quality will never mold.

It is honor, 'tis priceless fame,
　That we try to win,
And for some great name,
　Go to the world's end.

TO J. P. P.

Whilst gliding o'er the tempestuous sea of life,
And though its broad bosom swells with strife,
And the fiery billows of sorrow roll,
Thou wilt ever be the life and guiding star of my soul,
Yea, thine image is engraven on my heart,
Never to be obliterated though soon we may part.

CITY LIFE.

What a humdrum this city life,
Of joy and strife,
This one to meet, that one to meet,
This face sour, that one sweet,
Oh! what a commotion on the street;
People of all classes there we find,
Seeking employment of some kind;
Either in labor or luxury to engage,
As Time ceases not his warfare to wage.

With an eye of suspicion, one looks at another,
As they step nearer, or from thee further.
In their estimation your value is fixed,
Though far from genuine, and sadly mixed
With error and blackened crime,
If but in the robes of silk you shine.

The monster of deformities are hid
Underneath empty appearance's coffin lid.

Know ye not, oh! vain egotistical passer-by,
That beneath the waters of the ocean lie
Hidden the most precious pearls of the deep,
Under its turbid waters they silently sleep?
Then how judge you, by empty outward show,
What a man or woman can or may know.
Remember, that the chaff floats on the wave,
While the diamond makes the ocean bed its grave,
That appearance always gives away a fool or knave.

TRIED FRIENDS.

Tried friends, they hold a sacred place,
That we kindly and fondly embrace,
In the secret chambers of our heart,
That will never be erased though soon we part.

But transient friends, like dew on the grass,
Ere the mid-day of life from the mind will pass,
Nor leave on our hearts a foot-print behind,
Not effaced from memory's mind.

TELL ME NOT LIFE IS A DREAM.

Tell me not that life is but an empty dream,
Filled with things that are not what they seem,
For as we gently glide down her silvery stream,
Behold her crystal waters how like diamonds gleam,
And the shadowy clouds lightly floating o'er us,
Are but passing shades to brighten the sunshine before us.

And though our bark may be tempest-tossed to and fro,
O'er life's surging billows both high and low,
Let us not in despair, give o'er to grief and care,
For after every storm, there's a calm to kindly share,
Like the "balm of Gilead," heal the time-worn scar,
Made by sin on the soul its beauty to mar,
No grief so great, but what a solace we may find,
If we'll humbly bow to the Savior of mankind.

Oh! tell me not that our life is but a dream,
That our world with millions of people teem,
For no grand purpose in vast eternity to fill.
Think ye, the one who bid the waters be still,
Who neither sought home nor dwelling-place here,
Would charge his followers be faithful, to never fear,
In a work which would perchance prove idle fiction,
And had he not known the obduracy of men's conviction,
Would have made the turbid waters of life smoother run,
Until in eternity's vast ocean their work was done.

DUTY.

Oh! when from the path of duty,
    We wander away,
And mar the soul of life and beauty,
    By sin and decay;
Could we but lift the veil of future years,
    And there behold
The many burdened sighs and bitter tears,
    By truth told,
And how we are laying them by in future store,
Day by day adding to them more and more,

Seeing no good in others to admire,
But gratifying our own selfish desire.

Methinks if our every act would more careful be,
    More thought require
To guide the tongue that often runs too free,
    And like a fire
Consumes the good, which with care it might have done,
    Had it been
By a wise counselor advised and properly run,
Thus the grand achievement of life would be won.
    But human will,
Thou selfish monster which no good craves,
And only for self, will buffet life's stormy waves,
Know thou wilt be on her rippling, flowing stream,
Only a bursting bubble, a passing dream.

"TELL ME WITH WHOM THOU GOEST."

"Tell me with whom thou goest,
    And I will tell thee what thou doest,"
        Is a gem that is old,
        But true as gold,
For men of like minds, seek their own kind,
    And if we will but open our eyes
    To see, and ears to hear the cries
    Of "Dame Nature's" voice,
    We'll soon rejoice in her choice,
        For on wisdom's plan,
        She teaches every man,
    The only true way of life to live.

"Tell me with whom thou goest,
  And I will tell thee what thou doest,"
    As kindred association
    Produce kindred approximation.
For a man of good deeds, sows good seeds,
  And through life will shun,
  The company of an evil one;
  For nature in harmony must dwell,
  If she would her grand work do well.
    And thou, O man,
    Art on nature's plan,
Whilst you dwell here, on earthly sphere.

THE FIRST SORROW.

Oh! my soul, cans't thou e'er forget
The first great sorrow thou hast met,
When the stars seemed in silence to fall,
And midnight darkness reigned o'er us all ?
Nay ! I can ne'er forget when the angel of death
First in my happy home blew his icy breath ;
And to the Father how earnestly I prayed
That his cruel band might be stayed—
That He would a mother's only child spare,
That we might her company longer share.

But, fond heart, thy pleadings were vain.
"Don't grieve ; you can come to her again,"
Was the response to thy call, from Heaven.
Sweet were those words in consolation given.
Blessed thoughts, precious to my soul,
Is the promise of meeting in the fold

Of Christ's kingdom our loved ones,
Where peace, like a river, through eternity runs.

Where no stifling sob, nor rising sigh
E'er pains the heart or tear stains the eye ;
No sad farewells spoken, nor parting kiss,
E'er comes to that beatiful land of bliss.

Then oh ! my soul, a little longer wait,
And soon thou canst, at the " golden gate,"
Meet your darlings that have gone before,
Where the music of their voices will nevermore
Their cadences sweet float away 'mid the air,
But linger sweetly on the ear forever there.

DOUBTING FEAR.

Happy is the soul that has no doubting fear,
No broken sighs, nor bitter tear,
No anxious thought for the morrow,
No dread of life's great sorrow,
But with the assurance of the Master's will,
Can rely on his precious promises to fulfill.

Happy is the soul that has no doubting fear,
That can in smiling nature his Master's voice hear,
Whose sky is clear, with no shadows drear,
To darken life's pathway while journeying here;
Who 'mid sunshine and storm alike rejoice,
For in them can recognize the Master's voice.

Happy is the soul that has no doubting fear,
No pangs of remorse, nor taunting jeer,
To pierce the heart with its cruel tear,

But in all nature's echoes wild can hear
Music in the rustling leaves and rippling stream,
Which makes the melody of life a happy dream.

Happy is the soul that has no doubting fear,
But in life's pathway will join in the cheer
Which Nature kindly offers her children here.
The budding flower, the yellow leaf scar,
Teach us that blooming youth and golden years
Will alike be refreshed by heaven's crystal tears.

THE LOST FLOWERS.

[Dedicated to the memory of Lura and Jennie Perkins. Lura
Perkins departed this life June 11, 1869, aged 18 months
and 20 days. Jennie Perkins departed this life October 30,
1883, aged 12 years, 3 months, and 22 days.]

Ever in life we are amidst death,
No flower escapes his icy breath,
Though we live, yet we must die ;
Though we smile, yet we must sigh.
All earthly pleasures have their pain,
Clouds and sunshine will come again.
He that gives can take away—
When He commands we must obey.

And out of seven precious flowers
He gave me to adorn earthly bowers,
Two are transplanted to a fairer soil,
Where they bloom without blight or spoil.
And though others my lonely hours cheer,
Yet my angel darlings are ever near,
Whispering, "We are waiting, mother dear,
To meet you, drop not that tear."

TEMPERANCE CAUSE.

Ladies and Gentlemen, we have assembled here—
I hope not only to meet an expected compeer,
But something in behalf of our temperance cause,
Whether or not it meets with everybody's applause.
Let us not ourselves mockingly deceive.
Stand idly by to criticise what we believe,
To be our friends' failure and weakness,
But in a noble quiet spirit of meekness
Pass their imperfections silently by—
Not with a frown or a face awry.

People expect a great deal more from others,
Especially from strangers and their mothers,
When they themselves could do no better,
Neither in plain words nor in letter ;
And as I have been solicited to write
Something for your entertainment to-night,
I thought perhaps I could only try,
And if my essay was simple and dry
You might properly consider the source
And you would not be disappointed, of course.

Think not strange if I should fail,
And with cowardly fear turn very pale,
When I attempt to very plainly speak
Of our temperance efforts here so weak.
As you all are ere this time fully aware
That our frail efforts doth surely declare
The interest we take in this affair.
For we ought no reasonable pains spare
To make our Social lively and pleasant
And instructive to all our friends present.

Remember, the span of life seems scarce begun
When lo! we see its setting sun.
Then let us do all the good, while we can,
For our friends and fellow-man.
Oh! then let us all be up and doing,
With gentle actions and kind words wooing.

Save the erring youths of our land
Through the hallowed influence of our temperance band;
Let not one for another stand and wait,
But join in the army, soon and late
Let us in earnest battle for the right.
Whate'er we do let it be with all our might,
For there is none of you so weak and blind
But what have your influences of some kind,
Either for good morals or evil ones
That will either raise or lower men's daughters and sons.

Oh! then let us strive with unceasing care,
And never by example the footsteps of youth ensnare,
But ever look forward to the good we may do
If we prove faithful workers tried and true.
Let not false pride and vain glory
Hinder you from telling life's true story.

Tell it in your own simple way—
Care not for what others may say.
For, our friends' faults, with our own,
In a knapsack across our shoulders are thrown—
Theirs, in the front, plainly to be seen;
Ours, on the back, hidden behind a screen.
Remember our lives are what we make them,
That for evil or good our friends must take them.
Then let us, while sojourning here,
Do all the good we can, without a fear

Of what others about us may say.
Why need we care? Can they,
With their idle gossip make anything true,
No matter how much boasting they do?

It only shows a weak place in their brain,
Does us no harm but gives them the pain.
For pure waters will their level find,
And a pure thought will seek its kind.
You may travel the wide world all over,
And you'll never find a single rover
But what has in the somewhere a kindred mate
To share in the great future his own fate.
In life's garden you cannot pluck a single flower
But you can pluck another alike in beauty and power.
We do not for ourselves live alone,
And to make ours the only happy home.
For either friend or foe will remember you
According to the good or evil you may do.

And why not, instead of shadows, sunshine
Scatter abroad in the hearts of others to enshrine
The ties of golden friendship bound together
With the silken cords of love which nought can sever ;
But in the heart's bright home of affection,
Sweetly traced by fond Memory's tender reflection,
Will be an oasis in some friend's life,
Whilst toiling 'mid time-worn care and strife.
And though sorrow's great and mighty waves
Fiercely on life's stormy sea madly raves,
We are permitted to sail our tottering bark,
Surrounded by clouds and mists of miseries dark—
Mocked by the dim shadows of the past,
But safely in port we will anchor at last.

If we know no such word as fail,
Whilst in Hope's barge we bravely sail
O'er life's sea, fraught with many dangers,
Accompanied both by friends and strangers,
We will surmount every obstacle in our way—
Crowned with success enjoy the halcyon day,
When foes and friends in one cruise unite
In harmony to wrestle for the right.
And though the night be long and dark,
With hope in the palpitating heart,
Kindling warmth in the despair-frozen bosom,
Fills our soul with an inward heaven.

OUR FAULTS.

'Tis wondrous strange our faults we can't see,
When so plainly before us they chance to be;
For how often do we hear the girls say,
" Boys who chew tobacco every day
Can never be called our dear, nor honey,
Who thus foolishly spend their money."

But the girls chew gum all the while,
And spend their money with a smile,
And if we should their practice condemn,
They would say, " Mind your own business, you men;
As there is no harm in chewing gum,
Like drinking poisonous rum."

And you see if we happen, just for fun,
Once a month, to take a little rum,
They'll begin to whisper to each other,

" He'll never do, we must choose another,
    For we don't like boys who drink rum,
    And spend their money for that kind of fun."

Now they don't like for boys to drink rum,
    Neither do we like to see girls chew gum ;
    And if you'd have us mind our p's and q's,
    And our habits of life for us choose,
    Be sure you dot your i's and cross your t's,
    And somewhat the boys try to please,

As you are called the angels of the earth,
    Who fill our hearts with joy and mirth.
    But I hardly think the angels chew gum
    Any more than for fun they drink rum.
    And oh! how often we hear the sweet refrain,
" Oh! come, dear, please don't drink again ! "

Now, girls, if you must have your say
    About the boys and their bad way,
    Please allow us the liberty you take
    In repeating some mistakes you make.
    You say you don't like for boys to drink rum.
    Neither do we like for girls to chew gum.

But you say girls chewing nice gum
    Isn't half so bad as boys drinking rum.
    Perhaps not, but, oh! it spoils the features
    Of our fair angelic creatures,
    And from their pouting lips
    Their cherished sweetness sips;
    And now, girls, in all candor to you,
    If you'd have us reform, you must, too.

Then let us join in a chorus sweet,
    Whilst on the principle of reform we meet.

Let our sweet refrain in the future be,
From these evil habits we'll ever be free.
No more boys drinking accursed rum,
Nor girls chewing filthy gum.

TO THE VETERANS.

Pause, ye city fathers, ere you take action.
    Think you the railroad syndicate
Has built your cities and their attraction
    For this you must their cause vindicate—
Join hands with the monied monster to oppress
    Your citizens whose patronage has made
Your branches of business a financial success;

Thus enabling you to stand in the shade
    To devise ways and means for the defeat
Of the honest workingman's only plan
    To secure a living plain and neat,
By using with deathless grip the magic wand
    Invented by shrewd monopolists to secure
The hard earnings of the laboring man?

And think you not the time is at hand
    When the Almighty Father of this land
Shall not indignantly rise up and curse you,
    For " Vengeance is mine," saith the True,
Whose children you now shamefully pursue
    With the blood-hounds of old Jay Gould
To rob them, the flocks of his fold?

There is a curse written in the book of ages
For those who oppress the hireling in wages,
Who rob the poor of their honest labor,

And, with King Capitalist's mighty sabre,
Unmercifully cut the laborer in prices
To pamper the rich in their vices.

Vengeance is deep and, for a while, may slumber,
But when a reckoning is made for the number
Of those who joined in the King's love-feast
'Twill be sure not to mistake the beast,
For the devil is a coward, and in his fear
Will accidently in his hydra-headed form appear.

FRIENDSHIP'S FAREWELL.

Think not strange this magic spell
Should come o'er us when we say farewell,
For in true Friendship's fascinating way
Thou hast her chain linked day by day,
And though our associations here most sweet
Be severed, and we, perhaps, never again to meet,
Yet thy name will surely enkindle a flame
In those whom a thought from thee would claim.

'Tis said Friendship's ties must be broken,
That the bitter word, farewell, must be spoken.
The enchanted spell by poets has been sung,
But was there ever a garland of flowers hung
Over the altar of Love more pure and divine
Than that of friendship, or a sound sweeter chime
Than her lullabies softly floating in the air
Disseminating love into lonely hearts everywhere.

The golden links that bind our band together
Must, one, by one, now and then, kindly sever;

10

But these happy hours we'll ever fondly cherish,
For in Friendship's memory they can never perish,
But like the pearly dew-drops kissing flowers sweet,
Enlivens them with a freshness until again they meet
In the soft, stilly twilight hours of dewy embrace.
Though we now say farewell, yet thy accustomed place,
In memory will be refreshing till we again see thy face.

MAXIMS.

'Twas never clear, but always queer,
To my mind, how always, or very near
Those maxims many years old,
So many truths of late have told.
But "where there's a will there's a way,"
To accomplish most anything, they say.
This, in many instances has been true,
But experience has found times not a few,
When the will was determined, bound,
But the way could nowhere be found.

For "there's none so deaf as those
   That do not wish to hear,"
Save those, who nothing know,
   But to ridicule their compeer.

"It takes a thief to catch a thief,"
   Is very properly and truly said.
And 'tis every man's honest belief,
   For one measures another by his own head.

But as there is allowed exceptions to all
Common rules, both great and small,

There must surely be in this one,
For we know certainly there are some,
Who with a keen sense of perception
Cannot be mistaken in base deception.

" The birds of a feather flock together,"
Through sunshine and stormy weather.
Thus we see people of alike minds,
Congeniality in each other finds.

" Willful waste makes woful want,"
And makes many a stomach feel gaunt.
Though this lesson is taught every day,
How few people attention to it pay.

" A stitch in time always saves nine,"
And if practiced would save a mine
Of wealth for many that is lost,
Save the grief and tears it cost.

" Strike while the iron is hot,"
Is the way to make your spot.
Seize the opportunity while you can,
Should be the maxim of every man.

" Make hay while the sun shines,"
If you'd reach life's higher climes,
Never wait, nor procrastinate, till to-morrow,
For then neglect may bring you sorrow.

But " take time by the forelock,
Be like the old faithful day clock,
Make each moment count one,
Until life's great task is done.

TIME.

Down the silvery stream of time,
The music of the waters chime, chime ;
Mingling their sounds of joy and woe,
Whilst through life they gently flow.
Let thine ear catch the music sweet,
And thy voice its choral echoes repeat,
Harmonizing the tender chords of the soul,
Whilst through eternity's ages they roll.

THERE'S NO PLACE LIKE HOME.

"There's no place like home, sweet home,"
Where love and contentment around it roam,
Where peace and harmony with its inmates dwell,
Where merriment doth ring like a silver bell.

Home is where our associations are most sweet,
It is where our best friends we meet;
Home is where from perplexing scenes we retire,
Where we meet the smiles we most desire.

Home is where innocence should always dwell,
Charm its inmates with its magic spell,
No deception should ever be allowed to enter there,
But truth and purity reign everywhere.

Home is our sweet haven of rest,
Our pleasures with those we love best;
There let our joys unmixed and true,
Be found a jewel in all we say or do.

There's no place on earth like home;
After many a vain and fruitless roam,
To the weary-worn pilgrims found,
Its name to the ear awakens the sweetest sound.

Home, oh! how many bless that dear word,
'Tis the sweetest name that was ever heard;
Its many precious memories dear to the heart,
The sunshine of life forms the greater part.

YOUTH AND BEAUTY.

Youth and beauty must fade,
All through sorrow's vale must wade,
For none can the mighty hand
Of cruel Death's terrors withstand.
The beauties of every flower,
Must yield to its mighty power,
Must fold its leaves in death,
As it exhales its balmy breath.

Youth and beauty in every age,
By modern poet and ancient sage,
Have been praised in every song,
Amid earth's mighty throng;
Youth and beauty twin sisters are,
Their glories, like a shining star,
With love's flame illume the soul,
Disperse the gloom of the ghostly ghoul.

Hand in hand, youth and beauty
Loudly call for love and duty,
Their mission on earth to fill,

Whilst journeying life's rugged hill;
The morning goes, the evening comes,
A few more rising and setting suns,
Then man's work on earth is done.

BOOK OF NATURE.

The great book of nature lies open to all,
But, oh ! how few heed its call,
How few read its pages so as to understand
The many mysteries developing over our land.
The tiny bud opening, and full-grown leaf
Which adorns the gay flowers of the heath,
Is but the type of infancy, into manhood grown.
And the autumn leaves, in their sad monotone
Are fit emblems of manhood ripening in age,
That in nature's book, is written on every page.

TO AN ABSENT FRIEND.

May your skies of pleasure ever be clear,
Unobscured from disappointment, sad and drear.
May your future hopes grow brighter
And your burdens, as they meet you, lighter.
In a land of new prospects before you,
May life's shadows pass lightly o'er you.

May you think of the school girl left behind—
May she occupy a wee place in your mind ;
And in your happy moments think of me,
For you know I would love there to be.

I hope you will excuse my brief letter—
Perhaps the next time I will do better.

I know you can with propriety excuse,
For so small a request you can't well refuse.
Be sure you again very soon write
To me, if 'tis but this eve or to-night.
I will close my sheer nonsense now
By wishing you pleasant dreams, anyhow.

IGNORANCE.

'Tis said that "ignorance is bliss,"
But give to me none of this ;
But instead a noble, manly man,
Who pursues wisdom's true plan,
And a noble, womanly woman,
Who chooses but wisdom for her yeoman.

But siege, landlord or lady,
On the bright side, or the shady,
Come out with an honest profile,
Either with a jeer or with a smile,
And be what you pretend,
If 'tis not a great Godsend.

Be the woman or man,
On nature's original plan ;
In truth, be the best you can,
For since the world began,
So many changes have been made
Since Adam and Eve were forbade

From the tree of knowledge to eat,
Wherein they lost their seat
In the beautiful Eden fair.
Yet they were forced to go,
Where, they did not know ;
But in their unhappy flight,
We have surely lost sight
Of the true original erudite.

KNIGHTS OF LABOR.

This paraphrase which forms the name,
Of your order ascending the hill of fame,
Is fraught with a significant meaning,
For in our vocabulary of literary gleaning,
We find, you know, Knight means hero,
A champion, not a vile misanthropic bravo.
Then strive to be all your name implies—
Heroes and champions, both good and wise.

Hurrah! ye Knights, be ye men of valor,
Let your acts, like the noon-day sun, without pallor,
Beam with such a force that your foe
Cannot be mistaken, but will surely know,
That you are close on to the right track,
And can no longer by his games of quack,
Be humbugged in rotten politic scheming,
Upon which the political staff is leaning.

Beware of those enfranchised heartless designers,
Who when in power become your maligners,
And with contempt scorn the name of labor,

Though it be his very next door neighbor,
And the rudder which prevents his ship
From sinking, and gives him the grip,
The monied grip, he so much desires,
And for which his mind so nobly aspires.

Then ye gallant Knights your ships steer,
Carefully watch, the breakers to keep clear;
For methinks I hear their tumultuous roar
Come dashing to the surf-beaten shore.
But fear not breakers. nor stormy weather
While you in harmony dwell together.
Let no trifle cause dissension among you,
And thus give your foe a chance to wrong you.
[Please don't refuse to kindly excuse,
And not abuse, a thoughtless muse.]

EARTH'S BEAUTIES.

Beauties rare, with delight charm the eye,
Fix the soul on their Author beyond the sky,
Music sweet, with rapture charms the ear,
And fills the soul with a divinely cheer.

And though the loveliest flowers must decay,
Yet spring-time will again, in vernal array,
Bring others as fair and beautiful as they,
To bloom in the floral queen's month of May.

So when we gently pass down life's stream,
Our earthly career will then, like a passing dream,
Have floated away, and others will be
In our barks adrift on life's " fitful sea."

MUSINGS.

This lovely eve my musings I transcribe,
While alone by the humble but cheerful fireside.
Precious memories sweet, of pristine days,
Come flitting by, like the genial rays
Of the summer sun, in splendor arrayed.
Glowing in my bosom, loved forms are portrayed,
When we wandered together through the woodland glens,
Culling sweet flowers, watching the little wrens.

But ah! 'tis needless for such a delusive dream,
With fancies that are not what they seem,
To fill my mind or disturb my brain.
But awake, my soul, from this romantic strain,
For life's shadows silently around thee steal,
And soon for eternity will thy destiny seal.
But away, thou unwelcome visitor from my mind,
And seek some place of a kindred kind.

GOLDEN MORN.

Golden morn in loveliness all aglow,
  Is the prettiest scene in this life.
Tiny flowers with sparkling dewdrops overflow,
  Banishes from our mind worldly strife.

All nature is smiling in love divine,
  For bright Aurora is decking the east,
And 'round his golden face the heavenly rays shine,
  Giving light to every man and beast.

Golden morn is the glorious birth of day,
  But soon will by the dark shadows of night,
Hide her ample robes of beautiful array,
  And shut in her glories so bright.

Golden morn with all her beauties so cheering,
  Art like human life, a short-lived flower,
Blooming into beauty and sweetness so endearing,
  Then at eve passes away like a shower.

LIFE'S OCEAN.

Whilst on life's broad ocean we are sailing,
Drifting amid the many smiles, and sad bewailing,
We find that in the bright sunshine many shadows fall,
And where they are least expected by us all.
Though many voices are cheerily ringing in the hall,
Dark shadows are silently creeping upon the wall.
But if 'twere not for the gloomy darkness of night ;
We could never know the sunshine of life so bright,
For our earthly skies can ne'er be so fair,
But a cloud may cast its shadow there.

Out on life's broad ocean so grand,
Wafted on this wierd, uncertain strand,
Tempest-tossed- a wayfarer on the billowy wave,
The stormy clouds of care and grief to brave—
Soon, soon thy frail bark will land thee o'er
"Life's fitful sea," on the ever-beautiful shore
Of eternity's future realm of dreamy land,
Where the many wonders on the gleamy strand
Will doubtless in a strange surprise remind thee
Of the many, many scenes left behind thee.

TRIBUTE OF RESPECT.

___

TO THE MEMORY OF MAY IRVIN.

___

Days, weeks, months, and years have past,
Lo! another flower is plucked at last,
A rosebud severed from its mother stem,
No more to beautify the walks of men.
Fate decreed this rosebud should bloom
In brighter climes than this earthly gloom;
For 'twas too fair to adorn an earthly bower—
That earthly cares should cull this flower.

Hence 'twas transplanted in Eden's garden fair,
To ever bloom 'mid the choicest flowers there,
To be a companion of the loved sister gone before,
An angel of light on the ever-beautiful shore
Of eternity's ceaseless ages, pure and bright,
Where no cloud of care can ever veil their light,
But ever live in love's glow of golden sunshine,
The home of the soul's sweetest seraphic clime.

And though you feel that your darling is gone,
Remember, she has only entered the eternal dawn
Of sunshine and happiness in a fairer land,
To swell the chorus of the children's happy band,
And though your tears may fall and blind you,
Though the everyday scenes oft remind you
Of your own darling child, sweet little May,
Yet remember she could not here always stay.

Remember she has paid the debt,
That must be by all earthly pilgrims met,
Sooner or later the time must come

When the weary traveler's work is done.
Then, when your heart sighs for the loved one,
Whose toils are now over, and race is run,
Know ye, that your time may be near
When you must before the same tribunal appear.

Oh! then may you feel that while you live,
This earth can never true joys give;
That earth is only designed a temporary home
For the weary, worn pilgrims, as they roam
On their journey to that better land,
Where they may meet, on the silvery strand,
The long-lost loved ones, in a fairer clime,
Where is known no death nor days decline.

HOMEWARD SAILING.

Homeward we are sailing on the ocean deep,
Rocked by the waves, by the winds lulled to sleep,
To dream of loved ones whom we shall meet,
On the coming shore with a fond welcome sweet;
Kindred hearts will there unite in a long embrace,
Nevermore by Death's rude alarms be torn apace.
To the new-born soul sweet will that welcome be,
When from earthly trials and troubles ever free;
'To share with loved ones joys of an eternal morn,
Where noon-day ne'er passes, nor night e'er comes,
No dread nor fears, of what the morn may bring,
But ever in the present glow of happiness sing.

Homeward bound, we are cruising seaward,
A bird of passage on the wing drifting leeward,
-Our barge dashing o'er the waves rising high,

The mists and shadows that come o'er our sky,
Ever bid us be watchful for breakers are nigh,
That while in life we live, in death we must die.
With the ever-shifting scenes of life before us,
The passing clouds and flitting sunlight o'er us,
Impress upon the mind a thought full well,
That life is a passing dream, a broken spell,
Which time and tide can alone reveal
In eternity, its mysteries, its future weal.

TO GERTIE.

How lonely, dear jewel of my heart's delight,
To be so far away from thee to-night,

But whilst at home in blissful repose,
    My heart beats happily, my thoughts far away,
And for my lovely one my heart o'erflows
    With joyous hopes, while awaiting the day

When our hopes and fears may be united
In the holy bonds of purest love plighted,
Be sealed with the only genuine, the marital vow,
To ever love and cherish as you do now,
When frosted the hair and wrinkled the brow—
Will then your thought so much love allow?

When this manly form from age grows thin,
The cheeks all hollow the eyes all dim,
    Will your love be the same for me then?
Yea, methinks its flame will as brightly burn,
To welcome a fond smile or a happy return.

BE ORIGINAL.

To be original, is to say your own words,
    And to think for yourself at best,
To raise and kill your own birds,
    With your own stones from their nest;
For to steal words, is the same as birds,
    Caught from another man's barn.
But how can we avoid using words,
    That are not a part of somebody's yarn,
Though your ideas be original, yet in your say,
    You must repeat what others have said,
In prose and rhyme long before your day.

TO THE MEMORY OF JENNIE A. PERKINS.

Jennie, my own darling one,
Thy labors on earth are done;
No more will thy smiles so sweet,
Our saddened hearts lovingly greet,
For thou hast over the shining strand
Passed into a brighter, a happier land,
Where methinks thy angelic voice I hear,
Like sweet music borne on mine ear,
By angels whispering softly, "Never fear,
For your loved one is always near,
Anxiously awaiting the happy time,
When you'll meet in a cloudless clime,
Where sorrows never, never come,
Where the grand life of eternity is begun,
Where love never, never grows cold,
Nor the youth ever grows old."

A RIDE ON THE ACCOMMODATION CAR.

I am writing as the thoughts occur to me,
On my way to Dallas, riding on the M. K. & T.,
The old accommodation, rocking and jostling along,
Crowded, jammed, and packed with a merry throng,
Some talking, some laughing, others wildly staring
With eyes and ears open, minutely comparing
Scenes and notes as they reach the eager ear,
Surprising the eye, and amusing to hear.

Oh, this weary waiting, watching, and not knowing,
How long you must stay, nor how soon you're going;
How dreadful the suspense, when a gazing stock
For forty pairs of bright eyes, what a shock
To be scanned and measured from foot to head;
To be talked about and hear nothing 'tis said.

For we find by sad experience that nowadays,
People you meet have many and various ways,
To estimate both your morals and finances at once,
As your appearance either suggests a scholar or a dunce,
Which naturally creates an anxious desire to know,
What kind of a thought on you they'll bestow.

But fie! 'tis foolish, why should we blush or care,
For other people's thoughts or rudely stare,
If we be all right, and with no error share.
Why need we a thought lose or a moment spare.
But now the iron horse blows his whistle again,
Snorting and puffing, moving us on again;
No more time to write, but quietly meditate,
As we are jostling along at a lively rate.

YOU MUST EDUCATE.

Ho! ye Knights of Labor, you must educate,
And never your humble abilities over-rate,
So far as to forget and ostentatiously undertake
To advise the excellency, your lordly magnate,
Nor insult his honored dignity with a petition
To right the wrongs of your humble condition,
As you now unmistakably occupy the position
In which he evidently intends you to remain;
Never to murmur, never to complain,
But quietly submit to his individual gain,
As you Knights surely have not the brain,
To successfully compete with your gigantic foe,
Nor able your row in life to hoe,
Without his gifted counsel in the shade,
To tell you how a fine living is made,
While you through the mud and slush wade.

Be sure to pick your own bones, and not feast
On the dignified carcass of some other beast.
For I see some newspapers they diffuse
A deal of bitter venom, with jeers and spews,
About what the Knights should and should not do,
Strictly their own business should attend to;
And in politics they should by no means dabble,
As no good thing can come from such a rabble;
For it takes more brains, you certainly know,
Than a one-horse editor or a Knight can bestow,
To make Uncle Sam's government successfully go.

But be of good courage, we have been told
That Grant, Lincoln and the great men of old,

Were once poor men who worked for their gold,
The same as you, in the heat and the cold;
And if they had no brains when poor,
They found them at the rich man's door.
So this is the point you should look after,
Secure your rights, and things will go " safter."
Have your money in your own pockets,
Then you can throw your own rockets.

And not only your rights simply demand,
But be sure you have them at your command.
For 'tis in the workingman's power of to-day,
To make light-fingered officials feel his sway.
Then be up and doing, hoist your flag,
Be determined, let not your energies lag
In the contest for right, as error must fall,
When true principles unmasked make their call,
Base frauds must inevitably go to the wall.

'Tis not for the lack of energy or brain,
That the laborer asks his competitor to explain
The technical terms in various transactions used,
But for the want of time which he is refused
By his monied master, thereby much abused,
In not having acquired the necessary information,
To carry him successfully through life's station,
Now we want to have a change, a reformation,

Wherein a poor man's son may have a chance,
In the mighty career of the world's advance,
To keep an even race with his fellowman,
In life's battles on an easy, equitable plan.
Then, my friends, you need not distress yourselves
About our brains: we'll try to take care of ourselves.
As for our abilities, the future must decide.

If the Knights will only stand side by side,
Victoriously o'er the sea of contest they'll ride.

Then, ye gallant Knights, guard well your posts.
With the armor of right you'll conquer your hosts.
Then be ye valiant in the task you have begun,
Work from the early rising to the setting of the sun.
Be only faithful and the victory can be won,
For in unity the grand work can be done.

I will now close, by asking you to excuse
This simple effusion; you surely can't refuse,
When I have only said what I meant,
And sent it to you with good intent.
If it gives you any pleasure and no pain,
You may, at some time, hear from me again.

EARTH A WILDERNESS.

This earth 's but a wilderness drear,
And we but pilgrims traveling here,
Journeying on life's rugged road,
To man's sure and final abode.
When 'mid life's trials weary and worn,
Our hearts grow dreary and forlorn,
How sweet to pluck a beautiful flower
By the wayside, from a rural bower,
And leave its thousands blooming there,
Shining in pearly dewdrops fair,
Refreshing other pilgrims on the way,
To their eternal home of endless day.

This world 's a wilderness of sin,
With temptations without and within;

Temptations without to snare the feet,
Temptations within to poison the sweet
Of the soul so beautiful and fair,
Divinely created a heavenly image to bear.

The cheery smiles in life we meet,
The merry voices to the ear so sweet,
Are but refreshing dewdrops from heaven,
A balm for the wearied soul given.
O then let a smile instead of a frown,
Be the brightest jewel in thy crown;
Let the ringing laugh, the merry lay,
Cheer the weary traveler on his way.

FRIENDS WE DO NOT WELL.

Behold, my friends, we do not well,
 Whilst we are wasting time;
Sinners are dropping off in hell,
 Amidst their awful crime.

Let us arise and go tell the war,
 To the havoc hold of king,
That one and all, both great and small,
 May of his glories sing.

If we should wait another day,
 Some mischief great may come;
So then arise and haste away,
 To call poor lost sinners home.

From porter let the news be heard
 In the palace of the king,
Elisha's God has kept his word,
 And thus provisions bring.

BE CAREFUL HOW YOU SOW.

As the tree falls so it must lie,
  Youth well spent, in age brings no sigh,
Live to-day, for to-morrow you may die.
  Look well to the future, it draweth nigh.
Oh! then let us our time well improve,
  And for future use lay in store,
Good deeds guilty conscience cannot reprove,
  But will beautifully bloom in eternity evermore.

Oh! remember that our lives, like the grass,
  And the tender flowers of earth's field,
Must wither and from the stage of action pass,
  To unknown spheres, our fruits there to yield.
Oh! then be careful how you sow,
  For in this earthly career you are seeding
The fields of life here below,
  To bear fruit for your final reaping.

ILLS OF LIFE.

Of all the ills of life to bear,
There's none so rough, nor hard to wear,
As the one which falls to the portion,
Of a fair young girl wrecked on love's ocean.

No matter who's to blame, 'tis the same,
She reaps the fame, and bears the name
Of a starch, staid, prim old maid,
Just because you're afraid and delayed
Your passion to disclose and propose.

Oh! why then, young men,
Will you dare, the rose so fair,
To leave alone, blooming on the stem,
There to wither and fade, to an old maid,
Just because you're afraid and delayed
Your passion to disclose and propose.

Remember, young man, the best plan
Is always for you in everything be true,
No matter if 'tis for fun, to make a pun,
Let no one otherwise think it done,
Just because you're afraid and delayed
Your passion to disclose and propose.

THE FAR-OFF SHORE.

There is a home, on a far-off shore,
    Where weary pilgrims rest,
    An eternal home for the blest,
Where life's changing scenes come no more.

In that beautiful home, on the far-off shore,
    Where the orange blossoms we love,
    And the cooing of the turtle-dove,
Brings no sigh for the loved ones gone before.

For in that beautiful home, on the far-off shore,
    We'll freely drink with those we love;
    The only true joys found above,
Flowing from the eternal fount of happiness evermore.

In that beautiful home, on the far-off shore,
    Where the volumes of music sweet,
    Swell with enchantment, their echoes repeat
The musical voices of loved ones evermore.

Oh ! that beautiful home, on the far-off shore,
  Where the myrtle and the ivy bloom,
  Where love's sunshine dispels the gloom—
Is now the home of the loved ones gone before.

Oh ! that beautiful home, on the far-off shore,
  Where the pilgrims are ever landing,
  Across Jordan's silvery waters stranding,
Safe at home to dwell in peace evermore.

MY DREAM.

One night I had a dream, weird and wild ;
  I dreamed of my youthful, happy days
When the syren song of the tempter had beguiled
  My wayward footsteps into his wicked ways.
I dreamed I went a shopping 'round the town .
  In search of a bargain ; I went from store to store,
Selecting among the goods thrown from shelves down,
  And found many things which tempted me sore
To deal falsely by saying I could buy them cheaper,
  When I had no place found them half so low,
Nor so beautiful, and in designs no neater.

But to gain my point, I thought, you know,
  'Twould be no wrong, just this time a yarn
To weave, in order a few dimes to thus save,
  Wherewith stockings to buy instead old ones to darn.
For it seemed a long journey then to the grave,
  And plenty of time we could have to repent
Of all our little misgivings, stories, and sins,
  Ere death by father Time would be to us sent,
Or the trophies of despair o'er us its victory wins.

But "Nay," said the merchant, " we can't sell lower,
　As we are now disposing of our stock at cost,
And know that you can't do any better next door,
　But miss a bargain and thus your time be lost."
But selfish humanity chagrined at the thought
　Of a failure, other adventures wildly sought.
For the devil had me now under sway,
　And led me on a poor captive at his will.
So methought to a larger house I would go,
　Just across the square, and there make my bill.
No sooner had I started than I spied below,
　A horseman, dashing wildly up the street,
Which turned my course to avoid a collision.
　Stepping upon a pavement of marble so neat,
Mounted upon white marble pillars, pleased my vision.
　Entranced, unwary I strode along this narrow walk,
When to my surprise a girl I chanced to meet.
　Now methought what shall we do to prevent a balk,
We must either pass or make a retreat.

To do either, seemed a desperate struggle or blow,
　As the walk was both narrow and high;
Yet we had no time to wait but onward must go.
　It seemed there were posts every few feet near by,
That we might in necessity catch to and hold,
　While the other carefully passed on their way.
So we grappled round the post with an effort bold,
　And thus made our pass without further delay.

But the devil's road seemed a hard one to travel,
　For no sooner was this difficulty passed,
Than another came up still harder to unravel.
　Thus all along the journey was my soul harassed,
For lo! to my horror, I now came to a burning post,

The blue blazes wrapping themselves 'round in a mass,
Would turn me back, or my hands roast.
I pondered a long time ere I concluded to pass,
For it seemed so far to turn back on the road,
Over which I had come with difficulty before,
When I was now only a few paces within the abode
Of the place to where I was going, a wholesale store.

So calling up my courage, I quickly passed on,
Sustaining no injury save blistering my fingers.
But oh! horrors, what does this mean? Another,
Yes, another blue blazing fiery post of cinders.
Oh! heavens, what must I do? I can't go further,
And now to be defeated, not to reach the goal.
Dark despair will hover o'er my return,
Prospects have fled, perplexities overwhelm my soul,
As I gaze back o'er the trials that I have overcome,
And was so elated with bright prospects near,
Heeded not the warnings of danger a prize to win,
And is not this defeat, my soul too dear,
Canst thou bear to be thus foiled and defeated by sin?
But lo! I see, oh horrors! I can't go any further,
For lo! I see just one more ahead in the path.
Woe to me, had I turned when to the first I came,
And retraced my footsteps from this wrath,
From whence they led me to this place of blame.

But oh! my soul, if thou couldst but bear
To pass those two fiery posts, which lie
As thine only barriers, thou wilt then be there.
Or wilt thou get thee back, the same trials to try?
And now, whilst the clouds of Satan o'er me hung,
My soul was almost tempted to turn once more,
From whence it had been lured on and stung

With remorse languishing and bleeding sore.
But the devil, with his intrigues of old,
  Said, "Thou foolish coward, look ahead of you,
And see that you are almost within the fold,
  Retrace not your footsteps, but onward pursue,
For the prize is ahead for you to secure."

Oh! what a struggle between death and life!
  Lo! I've met my sorrow in the path of sin;
Onward or backward! I must end this strife—
  I can't tarry here—I can but lose all or win!
With fear I seized the monster post in haste,
  And was soon over this terror, yet there lay
Another, the last, so methought no time to waste,
  And with an almost crazed, frenzied mind,
I took hold of the last and third fiery post,
  And though my hands burned, yet I thought to find
A healing balm, a panacea among the inviting host,
  Who seemed to beckon me on with words so mild.
A handsome structure now stood just before me,
  Only a few more steps—oh, horrors! am I wild?
What's this burning heat that comes all o'er me?
  For verily I had stepped upon a platform that led
From the pavement to the house I had so long sought,
  When a burning heat from beneath ascended to my head,
My whole being seemed in a fiery steam wrought.
  When in agony I cried, "O, God, have mercy in despair."
A fiery nymph from the realms of old Pluto said,
  "Open the door and let her in, for 'tis but fair;
She has come the way of all others who in sin are dead.
  For there's not a soul in hell to-day but came
On your road, and was surprised to stop here.
  And was, like yourself, led on unawares by the same

Voice of procrastination—plenty of time, never fear."
"Oh, my God! have mercy," I pray, "for this I can't bear!"
"But you must," said the fiery nymph, "endure this,
  Like others have done, in this dark despair.
You had your warnings, that a hell you might miss,
  But like many others you heeded not the signal 'Danger!'
For those burning posts were warnings set for thee—
  Were put there to turn back the thoughtless stranger."

"Oh, my God! I tried to hard at the second to flee;
  Oh! my soul struggled so hard, but it seemed a long
Journey to retrace my steps back o'er the road,
  When I could see just ahead the merry throng,
And never thought of coming to this dreadful abode."
  "Nay," said the fiery nymph, "there's not a soul to-day
In hell that ever thought they'd come here,
  In regions of darkness forever to stay.

"Every sinner has his warnings of this place
  In time, if he will but hear he can it shun."
My warnings, like huge mountains, before my face
  Rose up to torture me for what I had done.
"Oh! God forgive me!" in agony I prayed,
  For I never thought of coming here."
"God never answers any prayers prayed in hell,"
  Said the fiery nymph, "nor dries any tear,
When you come to this land to dwell,
  Your preparatory days are, like your deeds,
A fixture of the past, no future in hell,
  A fixture of the past, in heaven no needs,
For when eternity dawns upon thy immortal soul,
  There will be no future, but an eternal present time,
As in the word present, will all mysteries be told,
  For changes can never come in the eternal clime."

Then my soul in agony sunk in dark despair,
As I cried, "Oh, my God! I am forever, eternally lost!"
My agony being so great broke the spell—nightmare!
Rejoiced 'twas but a dream, I cared not the pain it cost.

THE GREEN MANSION.

In a beautiful city, noted for its health,
Its numerous enterprises, fashion and wealth,
Was among many other palatial mansions seen
A mansion of artistical design, painted green,
Magnificently environed with floral beauties rare,
That with a sweet aroma filled the air.
Surely could aught but love dwell there?
Yea, a matron, kind and fair,
Who, had it not been for a boorish bear,
In the form of a husband, dwelling there,
Would often with the poor her kindness share.

And though this family who seemingly never knew
Aught but sunshine, yet shadows they threw
In the bright homes of the humble poor.
When an appeal was made at this man's door
For the needy, it was met by the stern reply:
"I have nothing to give; let them die.
Let them work out their own salvation,
For in the world's grand estimation,
If they die, they'll never be missed."
So all through life a bye-word like this—
"Let him die; he'll never be missed,"
Was his response to charity's call,
Be the pittance asked ever so small.

The site of this green mansion was on a street
Near a gilded saloon, where idlers chanced to meet,
Consequently their calls were common and frequent,
And at times would occur a sad event.

The story which we are about to relate :
Perhaps it was in the year sixty-eight,
On a cold, bleak wintry eve, the street
Was thronged with people, on flying feet,
Hurrying to and fro, out of the icy blast
Of pelting hail, falling thick and fast,
When a stranger was noticed, wending his way,
Deserted, alone, at the closing in of day ;
Slow and measured his steps were taken,
As if sad and friendless, perhaps forsaken.

He was pondering as he wandered along,
From the crowded streets and busy throng,
What he should do to shelter from the storm.
But the darkness of night covered his form,
And the thoughts of the lonely stranger,
His queer manner, and pending danger,
Were soon forgotten by those surrounded
With the comforts of home, that abounded
In everything which makes life so pleasant—
The past was soon lost in the joys of the present.

But the shades of night having passed away,
A cold, bright morn, ushered in another day,
And the busy crowds soon began to meet
Around the corners and on the street,
To relate the incidents of the weather,
When behold ! a crowd ran together,
To see something—'twas a lifeless form,
'Neath a window, frozen stiff in the storm.

'Twas the window of the green mansion fair—
Perhaps the cheerful light bade him go there.

But the inmates of that green mansion fine
Were allowed no thought, nor care, nor time—
Anything, to bestow on a tramp like this,
"Let him die, for he'll never be missed."
So in the pauper's grave they laid him,
A pine slab on the mound they made him,
Was all that marked his resting place—
His career was done, he had run his race.

But time and tide wait for no man,
Our life at best is but a narrow span,
Years have come and gone, and their changes made,
Many have seen their pleasures bloom and fade,
And the green mansion has reaped its share,
For its naked walls and floors all bare
Seem a tale of want and woe to tell,
A dream of happiness, a broken spell.

Like a sunbeam and shadow they fell,
The owner his green mansion was forced to sell.
Idle luxury, the wine-cup and wanton pride,
Upon his fortune had made a heavy stride.
The patient wife, in pleading terms vainly tried
To save him from ruin's wreck yawning wide,
To number its victims by thousands multiplied.
But ah ! a prey to grief, heart-broken she died,
And he, oh, where ? a beggar on the pitiless street,
Scorned by every one whom he chanced to meet.

When at last the sequel came, in a brief story told :
The sky was o'er-cast, the winds blew cold—
"Cruel cold !" said a beggar to his comrade bold.

"I wonder if there's any, in cottages neat,
Would hear my story if I'd it repeat?
I dare not try, I'll tell you why :
One night when the sleet was falling, the wind was high,
I thought I heard in the storm a faint cry,
It seemed a piteous moan, a broken sigh.
On raising the window, lo ! there I did espy
An old man, perhaps in age well-nigh
Three-score years and ten, feebly lie
Beneath my window, neglected there to die.

" 'Surely an old scamp, a beggarly tramp,
Wandered away from his miserable camp ;
Let him die, he'll never be missed,'
Said I, while a falling tear I kissed
From a loving wife's pale cheek,
Who, with a spirit lowly and meek,
Possessed a deep sympathy for human woes,
And would have relieved friends and foes,
If she could only have had her way—
But my will then must have its sway.
And oh ! it was I, not her, to blame,
For then, in my worldly, ambitious fame,
I would say, let them go as they came,
Let their condition be their own shame.

"But, stranger, would you know my story,
How in splendor and earthly glory
I once lived to my heart's content,
In idle luxury, which has my fortune spent—
The gaming table has its share,
And the wine-cup has a portion fair.
But my wife, where, oh where is she,

Since a beggar on the street I've come to be!
It seems to me I can faintly remember,
'Twas on a cold night in the month of December
That I wandered in darkness alone
On the deserted street in the search of home.

"When some one, catching me by the arm,
 Said 'Come this way, we mean no harm.'
 They led me into a dim-lighted room,
 Where everything seemed a dismal gloom.
 There they told me she was dead,
 But I did not realize what they said.
 For it seemed to be a cruel dream,
 To crush my heart with trials unseen.

"But now I know, it must be so,
 For many years I've wandered to and fro,
 In quest of something, I hardly know—
 It must be her sympathy I loved so.
 But ah! woe is mine, she is gone!
 Has gone to rest, and I'm left alone."
So to the wintry blast he bowed his head,
In a faint, low voice he quietly said,
"Let him die, he'll never be missed,"
Then in death the earth he kissed.

Thus ends the sad and tragic story
Of a youth who, in manhood's glory,
Sought to ride high on ambition's wave,
Gratified every wish his heart did crave,
But for the wine-cup, the enticing bowl,
He lost both his estate and peace of soul.

A VISION.

In the still watches of the night,
When the silvery moon threw her light,
Softly through curtains thin, around the room,
Chasing away the shadows of nightly gloom,
As the hours drearily passed away,
While I watched beside my little boy,
Our household pet, and fondest joy.

His fevered brow pressing my cheek,
With anxious thought, weary and weak,
I scarcely knew whether I slept or dreamed,
When a soft hand on my shoulder seemed
In a strange surprise to call my attention,
But thinking it might be some nervous invention,
As my efforts to scream awoke me,
" Perhaps," I said, " 'tis nightmare threatens to choke me.

Hastily I arose to ascertain the cause of this fright,
When I discovered 'twas but a vision of moonlight.
So thinking this must be only a dream, I said,
" How foolish," and beside my boy on the bed
I softly laid me down, and closed my eyes,
Methought, to sleep again, when in surprise,
I felt a light touch from the same soft hand.
Being awake, I had my feelings under command,
And said, " This must be, can only be, imagination,
Caused by excitement or nervous prostration."

When again by this unknown visitor another demonstration
Impressed my consciousness with a soul-stirring sensation,
Which seemed to take possession of my mind,

Saying, " Let us go back to the place and find
Where God first made his creatures, and man,
And see how he was created, and on what plan
Was he made to rule and govern the earth ;
For a ruler over the animal kingdom was he at birth."

First, let us look into the beginning of all creation, and
behold the great and infinite wisdom of our divine Creator, in
creating this grand universe.   Behold his power, when he called
forth out of the illimitable depths of darkness the marvelous
realms of light, and in the bright firmament above fixed the
blazing sun to give light and warmth by day, and the moon to
regulate the seasons thereof.   Behold, the starry host which
attracts the admiring gaze of millions of people, and absorbs the
most penetrating thought of learned philosophers and scientists,
and see their uses, and missions which they fill in the vast
expanse of heavenly space.   For many of the heavenly planets
have been noted as precursors of certain events by astronomers.
They say some planets denote war and bloodshed, some denote
earthquakes, storms and tornadoes, others denote peace and
prosperity, and they all have a signification, which men will, in
ages to come, understand what now seems to them earth's mysteries ; but he must gain this knowledge by labor, day after day,
as God has said, for man's transgressions he must labor for all
that he justly acquires.

And now I seemed to wander away in other fields of
thought, pertaining to my own affairs, when this secret possessor
of my mind would call me back, saying, Let us return to
where we left off.   After God had framed the world and its
planets, and placed them in their respective positions, to be governed by fixed laws, called laws of nature or natural laws, he
then called forth from the great fountains of the deep, and
caused the sparkling fountains to break forth from the hillsides,

flowing gently down through the valleys in living streams, for the refreshing of earth's creatures.

And God now looking out upon the earth, beholding its vast plains and naked hills, a waste of barrenness, caused a mist to rise and fall upon the whole face of the earth, which brought forth the springing of the grass, and all manner of herbs yielding seed after their kind, clothing the earth with a beautiful mantle of verdant greenness. Behold, the Author of all that is good, grand, and beautiful, how magnificently he displayed his infinite powers of beauty and taste, when he planted the beautiful flowers all o'er the hills and valleys, so profuse in varieties, that it is almost beyond human conception to conceive a correct idea of their different kinds and true characteristics, tinted with every hue, reflecting every shade imaginable—the bright red, the rich scarlet, the beautiful crimson, the pink, carnation, damask, and ruby, and the golden colors of yellow, orange, amber, and the delicate cream tints, the beautiful sky colors of blue, besides the many complementary colors of lovely shades in abundance, to ornament the valley gardens of earth.

Behold now this beautiful earth, man's paradisial home, with its blazing star shedding its transcendent light o'er its beautiful fields of fruits and flowers, invigorating them with its glowing sunshine of light and warmth, as it passes its allotted course in making the period of day, and sinks beneath the azure sky, when night veils earth's beauties in her sable garments of darkness, and the morning stars peering through her mystic veil sing together for joy, as the silvery moon rises in queenly majesty with her shimmering rays of lucid light, sweeping away the mys_ tic veil from o'er these beautiful scenes of silence.

Let us now, as we view nature in its primeval state, with no living creature to mar its unbroken scenes of loveliness, nor to enjoy its bounty and munificence, know that the Author of these things had a righteous design, with an authenticated purpose in view, when he created everything so good and beautiful, for we behold no evil things growing among the many useful and ornamental things of earth, no briars nor brambles, no thistles nor thorns find a place here. Nay, but this is a land of cooling shades and beautiful sunshine, where the silvery streams of cool waters gently wend their way through shady groves, through a land of fruits and flowers, unmolested their crystal waters rippling o'er their pebbly beds pursue their onward course. And as God looked out again and again, each day, to behold his creations, he was pleased with them and said they were good.

And not having yet created any living creatures to make use of the things of earth, he now created the beasts of the field to feast on the rich tender herbage of green pastures, and slake their thirst in the purling streamlets of cool sparkling water, and the flying fowls of the air to flit in the sunshine and shadows of leafy bowers, picking the luscious fruits which grow in abundance, building their nests whilst warbling their songs of love so free; and the fishes of the sea, the finny tribes of the sunny waters, sporting in the sunlight of heaven, all these had God created, but not man, and being pleased with all that he had created, he said, Let us now make man, and give him dominion over the earth and all of its creatures, that he may rule over them. Behold what a princely seat man is to occupy, to be a ruler over such a kingdom as this, a land of milk and honey, a land of ambrosial fruits ripening in successive seasons of the year, a delicious food for man and beast, and the beautiful birds of paradise in their gay plumage to delight the eye, and the sweet songster that warbles forth his sweetest songs of melody, to delight the ear, and cheer the heart of man.

> A land of fruits and flowers,
> A beautiful garden of leafy bowers,
> Where the birds of the air,
> In their rich plumage there,

Sing their songs of love,
Sweetly to their Maker above,
Where the bright sparkling fountains,
Gush forth from the rocky mountains,
In living waters gently flow,
Through the flowery vales below,
Where the creatures freely drink,
To quench their thirst, at their brink.
Could aught but love dwell,
Or a sweeter chorus swell,
In a lovely paradise like this,
Where all, all is pure bliss.

And this, was to be man's home, a home abundantly furnished with all that he needed to make him happy now, and in the ages to come. There was plenty to supply him in each and every age, as they passed down to him, for God knew in the beginning how he would create man, and what he would need in the future. So all things were created in the beginning for his use when the proper time should arrive, and the right season for its use so as to be beneficial to him; but God was to decide the time for its use, as he knew best when that time was.

As man was but a child in knowledge when created, and needed a father's advice and counsel to direct him, until he arrived at the years of maturity, accordingly God commanded man to obey him, as this was right for children to obey their parents, as they love them and know what is best for them. And God created man in his own image and likeness, that is, an immortal soul, to inherit eternity, yet not in knowledge, as that was only a principle feature, to be developed in the proper time, as the mind matured, and thus have been enabled to receive it; hence a fruit was placed in the garden for this purpose at the proper time, for the developing of man's knowledge.

Let us see wherein God created man in his own image and likeness. We will say when God created man, he created him in his own image and likeness, that is, with an immortal spirit, which must live through all eternity. And when he said, Let us make man in our own image and likeness, he meant evidently both in a literal and spiritual sense; therefore, while man was created an heir to eternity, partaking of this principle from his creator, he certainly must inherit some of his natural attributes from the same source. And as our creator was a ruler and his own counselor, and had the power to act for himself, therefore, in order to make man in his own image and likeness, he was compelled to make him a free moral agent to act for himself; consequently he was created a free moral agent and was placed in a condition to exercise this power, in a position that he might demonstrate the power or ability of a free moral agency, as there were two distinct influences surrounding their moral atmosphere, for the evil spirit, or tempter, existed before man inhabited this earth and was ready to put in his work as soon as possible. And God in his wisdom knew this, so he gave to them an early commandment that they should not disobey him, inasmuch as he had created them, loved them, and knew what was best for them to have, and as an indulgent father would for the love he bore for his children command them in a righteous way to obey him, for the sake of their own welfare and happiness, so he gave to them an early commandment, that if they would do well and be happy, they should not disobey him; if they did, what its sure consequences would be.

For a wise purpose, and through a righteous design, unknown to man, for he was then in his infancy, dressed in his swaddling clothes of earthly career, not able to comprehend the grand objects of his Creator, both the tree of life and knowledge were planted in the midst of this beautiful garden of Eden, man's earthly home, and of which God forbade them to eat, saying, "For

in the day that thou eatest thereof, thou shalt surely die." Thus
you see, they were to either obey or to disobey God's commands,
as they were free moral agents, to choose for themselves to keep
their Father's commands, and enjoy his favor, blessed with all
they needed to make them happy and contented in this their
earthly home, or to disobey God's commands, and receive the
rewards of punishment, which they so justly deserved; for this
was the only alternative left between God and man, the creator
and creature, as it is impossible for a being so wise and good as
God, to lie or to contradict himself. And when he says that he
created man in his own image and likeness, an agent to choose
and act for himself, we must admit, though he foreknew all
things, though he foreknew man's destruction by his disobedience, yet he could not stretch forth his hand and prevent man
in choosing the evil instead of the good, as he was his own agent
to choose and act for himself, and if God had interposed and
forced men to do right, he would, in thus doing, have destroyed
man's free moral agency and contradicted his own word and
work; hence man was left to act for himself. God loved man
and did what was in his power, as a just and righteous Father
could, to save him from his fall, in commanding him to shun the
evil (ere the devil had a chance to tempt him), telling him its
fearful consequences if he did not.

And shall we blame God, because man chose the evil instead of
the good, when he knew its dreadful consequences? God forbid.
Or shall we suppose that man had as much right to believe the
devil as he did God? For what evidence had he that the devil
would advise him for his welfare, as he had never before demonstrated any kindness for him. Then had man any evidence that
the devil would bestow a blessing which God would withhold
from him? None whatever, but he had every evidence that God
would bless him, as he had so often done before, if he would
obey his commands. But the devil was now ready, with his sub-

tile device, to put his work in. So he assumed the form of a serpent, in order to deceive the woman, saying to her, "that this fruit which God commanded thee not to eat, is good and pleasant, and will make thee wise as gods, knowing good from evil," and "thou shalt not die in the day that thou eatest thereof." This saying sank down deep into their hearts, and oh! what a fierce struggle ensued between life and death. They knew it was wrong to disobey their Father, yet the thought of being as wise as God, was a momentous thing; that it would be too grand, an achievement too glorious to miss. Perhaps they thought it would be worth dying for, as they could not realize to the full extent, all the horrors of death (or perhaps they reasoned with themselves like people do now, that God was too good to punish them), and now, being fully persuaded, put forth their hands and plucked the forbidden fruit (oh! what a victory for the devil, he has accomplished his fiendish design) and did eat, and their eyes of understanding now being opened, they began to realize what they had done, and hid from the Lord. But alas! foolish, erring children, thou couldst not hide thyselves nor sins from the Father, for when the Lord went out into the garden, in the cool of the evening, they had secreted themselves, to hide from him. But when God called to them, and asked why they acted this way, they answered, "Because they were naked," thus acknowledging their guilt. And the only reason they could give for their disobedience was, they had been by the serpent persuaded to eat of it, because the fruit was pleasant and good to make them wise. Consequently they transgressed the righteous laws of their Father, and thereby fell from their purity, entailing the great misery of evil upon all mankind. Had they rebuked the devil, as the Savior did, when he was tempted by him in the wilderness for the space of forty days, when the devil offered to give him power over all the kingdoms of the earth, if he would only bow down and worship him, who said, "Get thee behind me, Satan, for thou shalt only worship the Lord thy God, and him only shalt thou serve;" and if the woman had only said, "Get thee behind me, thou evil serpent, for the Lord our God, who gave us this beautiful garden of Eden for our home, and supplied us with all that we enjoy, commanded us not to eat of the tree of knowledge, for in the day we did, we should surely die. So go your way; and tempt us not to do that which we are forbidden," oh! how much woe and misery might have been avoided.

Now let us view the other side and see what man would have been, if he had not transgressed the laws or commands in eating the forbidden fruit of knowledge. Would he still have remained in blissful ignorance of God's creation? Or would man have acquired a sufficient knowledge of the creation as he gently passed down the silvery stream of time, to have fully met the demands of earth's progress in the ages which he lived. Yea, as they passed on, and on, down Time's rapid stream, he would have acquired sufficient knowledge to have answered all of life's purposes until the fullness of time would arrive, when he would be fully developed, matured in mind, a full-grown man (instead of a child), having learned all the natural laws of creation, his mind would now have been prepared for a stronger food, in the way of thought or mind matter; meat instead of milk could have been safely used, to his advantage. He would now have been too strong for temptation too overthrow him. And the Almighty Father, who gives out of his abundance to his children all they have need of, seeing the time had come when man was prepared for this knowledge, would have freely given it to him, and so enlightened him, insomuch as man would not only have known good from evil, but to fully understand and know the relationship existing between him and his Maker. Yea, all the mysteries of this life would have been solved, and they would have been truly wise and great, for the same truths of inspiration

which gives us the history of man in the garden of Eden, also
says there is a time and season to every purpose under heaven.
'Tis said, one truth explains or confirms another, and is always
admissible when both are substantiated through or by the same
authority. Then if we say there was such a place as the garden
of Eden, and the tree of life and knowledge was placed in the
midst of it, we must admit that they were put there for a purpose, and as there is a time and season to every purpose under
the heaven, there was evidently a purpose designed in the planting of the tree of life and knowledge in the garden of Eden, and
a time and season for its use. And as God tempts no man, it
was not put there for a temptation (as some foolishly suppose),
but through a righteous design, for the Scripture (Eccl. 3:1)
says, "To everything there is a season, and a time to every purpose under the heaven." Therefore, it is conclusively set forth,
a clearly proven fact through the divine teachings of the Scriptures, that both the tree of life and knowledge were planted in
the garden of Eden for man, as a blessing if it had been used at the
proper time and season, and did not require man's transgression
and fall to obtain it, but required his strict obedience to his
Father's commands, and patience in well-doing, until the fullness
of time had come, when God, seeing it would have been good
for him, would have freely given it, for he freely gives to those
who love and obey him, and withholds no good thing from them.
And we certainly must admit, as rational, reasonable and intelligent beings, that a great many things we know to be blessings,
which, if used imprudently at improper times, would prove very
injurious, and probably a curse to us. And would it not be simple in the extreme, for us to say, because we used anything inju-
diciously and out of season, and it proved disastrous to our well-
doing, that we could not help it when we knew better, and say
that God ought not to have placed in our way such things, as he
foreknew all things, and that he intended for us to do these foolish

acts, so that he might have an opportunity to punish us for them. And as some foolishly suppose, to show us his power to save fallen man, he placed the tree of knowledge in the garden of Eden, knowing that man would be tempted and yield, and thus give him an opportunity to display his power and goodness, by stretching forth his strong arm to save his people. Nay, I tell you, God had no necessity to resort to any such folly as this to demonstrate his infinite power, which surpasseth the understanding of mortal man; neither to curse us, in order to bless us afterwards. Away with such folly and sheer nonsense as this. Let God be true if every theory be false.

Now, let us illustrate the more powerful truths by the simple ones. What would you think of a woman who would persist in feeding to an infant fat meats, or bacon, because she was told it was good for man, to give him strength, and this infant boy, she thinks, needs strength and nourishment to make him grow strong and fast, and feeds it on a diet unsuited for its tender stomach, and thus deranges its digestive organs ; and if it does not destroy its life, makes it a miserable invalid? Does this foolish act justify her in saying that God was unjust for placing such a strong diet within her reach? Must he remove this blessing out of the reach of man, whom it was designed to bless, to prevent unwise and foolish mistakes? Nay, this meat at the proper time of life, and in season, would have been a blessing, instead of a curse.

So Adam and Eve made the same mistake ; they should have, in their infant days of earthly career, used milk instead of meat, and when the proper time and season in life had arrived, it then would have proved a blessing. We may use a thing unwisely, to our great injury, and find a timely remedy to alleviate or to modify the wrong, and thus prevent a total wreck of happiness or existence ; but would it not be the height of folly for us to say we were compelled to make use of injury in order to apply the remedy? So God prepared a timely remedy to save his erring children; yet it was not the design nor will of the Father for them to disobey or transgress his laws in order to apply the remedy for the evil. Nay, but it was man's own choice, as he was his own agent to act for himself, and fell a victim to temptation, the same that men do to day. The tree of knowledge was no temptation, but the syren song of the devil to which they listened, and thus became infatuated, was the temptation. We have just as much right to say that the kingdoms of the earth was a temptation set before Christ to tempt him as the tree of knowledge was put in the garden of Eden to tempt man, as the devil offered to give Christ all the kingdoms of earth to fall down and worship him, and, if such a thing had been possible, then they would have said God put the kingdoms here to tempt Christ—this is just as plausable as the other saying. The devil is man's tempter, not the things of the earth which God created for man's use and pleasure. But God so loved his people, whom he had created for a pleasure—though they had committed such gross sins, unreasonable sins, violated his righteous laws, which were only made for man's benefit, and great gain had he obeyed them, that he sent his only begotten son into the world to atone for man's sins, that he might be saved if he desired it, if not might be lost. For it is not the will of God that any man be lost, but his own acts, for by man's acts or works will he be justified or condemned. And we to-day are in the same position that our parents were, when in the garden of Eden. We are free moral agents, to act for ourselves. We can obey our Father's commands and reap eternal life, or disobey them and reap eternal death. For God is not responsible for man's sins, as he is his own agent to choose for himself, and if he prefers death to life, justice says that he shall have it, and the man who is lost hath only himself to blame, for he that will, can be saved, for the great physician is at hand ready to heal the sin-sick soul, if it will only accept the treatment.

Then, oh man ! why bring up false accusations against thy Maker? false theories to justify thyself in thy wickedness, when the loss sustained thereby is all, all thine ? Why not accept Christ thy Savior and be healed, and turn from thy sins and do the works of the righteous and live. For those who doeth the works of righteousness shall reap eternal life, but those who reject Christ and doeth the works of unrighteousness shall reap eternal punishment.

Then, oh man ! know ye, that God is justified in all things whatsoever he doeth, and it is his great pleasure that all men might be saved. Yet he can not force anyone to be saved, as God is just, and justice demands punishment for a violation of its laws. God is a righteous law-giver, and gives to all men alike. He is no respecter of persons. He looks at man's heart, not his appearance.

Now let us take man as he is by nature, and view him from an original standpoint, and see what kind of a creature he is. Man, in his views (speaking in a general sense) is a very one-sided creature, for he only looks at the side which pleases him best, and tries to measure God's justice by his own poor, misguided feel-ings, for man's judgment is more or less perverted by selfish motives, and self interest. But God, the All-Wise Ruler of heaven and earth, who knoweth the hearts of men, and needeth that none should testify unto him, is able to pass righteous judg-ment on all men.

Now let us see what kind of a creature man is, or what shall we compare him unto.

What kind of a creature is man? And what shall we liken him unto ? To demonstrate the character of man more fully to the mind, we will illustrate him by the simple natural laws of nature ; which every individual with a reasonable observation

can not fail to see the analogy. For instance, we will compare
man to a kind of fruit, or nut, with a kernel encased in a hard
shell. We will say that the kernel represents the spirit of
man, the shell the natural body. And though the shell may
to all outside appearance be very rough and unseemly, but
crack it open and there you often find a plump, well-filled,
healthy kernel. Then again, you may pick a nut with a smooth,
nice shell, and crack it open, and there, in all probability,
you will find an ugly, wrinkled, deformed, unhealthy kernel,
encased within this beautiful shell. So it is with man. You
cannot tell by his outward form what kind of a soul he has
within him. His form may be beautiful, his external nature
seem perfect, but his spirit may be sin-scarred and blackened
with crime, "a whited sepulcher, filled with dead men's bones."
Then again we often find, though the outward form of man may
seem uncouth and unseemly, yet there is something prepossessing
about him ; his soul, with its bright congeniality, seems to beam
forth with a divine inspiration, emanating from its divine Father,
speaking the true and noble sentiments which can only come
from the heart of a genuine type of humanity. For man is a
being of exponent parts, composed of two distinct natures.
mortal and immortal, "the seen and unseen." The mortal or
natural part of man, the body, the form which we behold with
the natural eye, like all the natural or visible forces of nature, is
the weaker part of creation, since we see the great combined
forces of unseen nature are greater and more powerful than the
visible. Hence we see the component parts of nature symbolizes
man. For in nature we find both a visible and an invisible creation. In man the visible creation is his body, the invisible his
soul. In nature the visible or external views of nature, and the
invisible power or forces of nature, which comes in the form of
tornadoes, and in its terrific fury sweeps everything before it.
Yet this monster, with his dreaded power, is to the sight of man

viewless; his disastrous effects are, nevertheless, most sensibly acknowledged. Therefore, with such demonstrations of power as these, we dare not deny their existence. Hence man is taught conclusively by nature that he is a creature of component parts, of mortality and immortality, the mortal body and the immortal soul, and as the unseen forces of nature conquer and subdue the natural, so shall the spiritual or unseen power of man conquer and subdue his natural or visible creation.

And how are we to know anything concerning the future state of man, only through the divine oracles of God, written by man through inspiration, and the teachings of nature? And if we would find out or solve the mysteries of man, we must be a zealous student of nature, for there we will find that all earthly creatures, though of very different forms, and created for varied uses, are more or less governed by the same laws of destination. For we have numerous instances of this law, of minor importance to that of man, the noblest creation of God, yet we can demonstrate the more powerful and wonderful creations with the minor ones. And for an illustration we shall use one among the most insignificant creatures in solving the mysteries of the more grand; in other words, to simplify the change or transformation of man into a future or higher life, beyond the dark portals of the grave, by the transformation of one of the insect tribes—for instance, the detestable caterpillar, which crawls through creation, subsisting wholly upon the green vegetation for its nourishment, changes its loathsome form into a beautiful butterfly, to bask in the glowing sunshine of earthly light, to cull the sweets from the fragrant flowers. So man, encumbered in this tenement of clay, heir to all the ills of life, crawls through creation as the miserable worm, until death, the transformation, makes him an heir to eternity, disrobes him of mortality, and clothes him with the light of immortality, to see and know as he is known.

If we will study nature and learn all of her natural laws, which govern all earthly objects as well as living creatures, we will find with an impartial eye that the divine Scriptures are in perfect harmony with the laws and teachings of nature ; and it must be absurd, to say the least of it, for a man to deny the truthfulness of anything because his feeble mind is not capable of comprehending it, as there exists so many things that we can't conceive their origin, yet we dare not deny their existence. 'Tis true that we may form an idea concerning their origin, but can we demonstrate it to any certainty? Conclusively, we cannot.

Earth's but the shadow of heaven,
Only a type of better things to man given,
While we travel through this shadowy land,
Pilgrims to a fairer and better land.
Then mistake not the shadow for the thing,
For wisdom will to her children bring
The true blessings they so much desire,
If their minds search and for truth aspire.

Then seek and you shall find the way,
It is open for all, who will come may.
O come, ye weary, worn travelers to-day,
While the sun shines make your hay.
Lay aside your burdens of doubt and fear,
Ere the clouds of sin obscure thy skies so clear.
For without substance shadows cannot appear,
But vanishes as your real life draws near.

We have but to look to see the love
Manifested to us by our Father above.
For think you of a single thing on this land,
That was created with thine own hand !
Nay, but all things you enjoy were given

To you in love, by your Father in heaven.
Though your joys and pleasures be mixed with pain,
The clouds will vanish, the sun shine again.

Then ye drooping souls, be of good cheer,
For soon you'll reach a land not so drear,
And as ye journey on, day after day,
Though trials and troubles meet you on the way,
Oh, lay your burdens down at night
At the foot-stool of Jesus, he is thy might.
He will guide and direct thee in the way
That leadeth thee to a home of eternal day.

Oh, let not the devil lead thee astray,
In saying that God has set in thy way
Temptations and trials too strong to bear—
Knowing thy weakness, thy soul to ensnare.
Nay, but thine only tempter is the devil,
Who seeketh to bring you down to his level,
And your inheritance of happiness to destroy,
By using the blessings God meant you to enjoy.

A PRIZE TO WIN.

We must bear the cross,
    If we obtain the crown ;
Be refined from the dross,
    To reach the fields of renown.
No prise is e'er won
    From the fields of fame,
No task is e'er done
    That we can e'er claim

As a conqest of honor secured,
But what perseverance has matured.

Then, as we trudge along
  Life's weary, toilsome road,
Where cares our pathway throng,
  And shadows darken our abode,
Let us not in despair despond—
  After every storm there's a calm,
And in the beautiful beyond
  We'll for every wound find a balm,
To heal our earthly sorrow
In the eternal sunshine of to-morrow.

The greatest inventions of man,
  The brightest lights that shine,
In the dark ages began,
  Only a spark gleaming in the mine.
Touched with the magic wand,
  Of ambitions, perseverance and toil,
Has brightened into a world most grand,
  A reward to the honest sons of toil.

PROSE DEPARTMENT.

HIGHER LIFE.

There is a higher life for man, a higher, a nobler life for us to fill; a higher life that we must attain to, or sink lower, as there is no level grade in life. We must either come up to the standard of a true man or woman, or sink beneath the dignity of one. Then let us ask ourselves the question, take it right home to our hearts, and try to solve the query as truthfully and intelligently as possible, and that is, What is life, and what is its true purposes? 'Tis not only to eat, sleep, and to live; nay. But methinks I hear some one say, It is to work, work, work, that we may have something to sustain life, for who can have anything to eat and to wear unless they work to make it. Some work with their brain to make labor for other people. This is the way the world wags anyhow. If you haven't the brains you must work for those that have. That is your own misfortune. You must not stop to inquire whether you have any sense or not, but just go straight forward in life, and you'll get through some way; you are bound to. There is a class of individuals who never look to one side or the other, perchance to see anything new, but go through life and never know anything outside of their work. So you see this class of people are what you might properly call common tools for other individuals who go up higher in life.

Do not understand me to say that work is degrading; far from it, for labor is both grand and glorious. But my friends, perhaps we do not in every sense of the word thoroughly understand what labor really is, as the word labor embraces a vast meaning, for there is not anything accomplished only through labor. If a man does not labor with his hands, he does with his brains, which is often more exhausting. The word labor is similar to the word life; they are synonomous terms. You know perhaps as much about one as the other. You think labor is to work, and to work is labor, and life is to live, and to live is life. To sum up the whole matter, there are a goodly number who do not really understand the true theory of either. "'Tis not all of life to live," "neither is it all of death to die," for if we fail to live to life's true purposes, eventually falling short of the great, grand and glorious position in the higher life of intellectuality, we have sadly failed to live our whole life, we have lost the best part of it. Oh! what grand inexpressible delights might have filled our souls in a pleasing transport of eternal felicity, had we but grasped the golden opportunities whilst within our reach. But ah! alas! with a goodly number—

> Those precious opportunities and happy days,
> Like the sun's beautiful golden rays,

Are fleeting and flown on speeding wings of endless time, conveying the news of sad disappointments and wrecked hopes to the invisible world of futurity.

"Neither is it all of death to die," as temporal death is only the gateway into a future world, where we will reap what we have sown in this life. If we have missed the grand and true purposes of life, we certainly will reap remorse and disastrous failures, whilst others who took hold of life's duties earnestly, and improved their talents in the golden moments as they were given to them, one by one, will then be enjoying a happy fruition in the glowing sunshine of eternity, reaping the delighted rewards of industry. Now is the accepted time. Delays are dangerous. They are highway robbers; they steal our time and often our life's happiness. Then let us be up and doing. Take time by the forelock. Make the best of life we can.

"For luck is pluck," I say,
And "where there's a will there's a way,"
And those who follow precepts true
Will make life a success all through.
'Tis our mistakes we make in life
That brings our care and strife.
For life, lived practically, is a scene
Of happiness and contentment, I ween.

For wherein does true happiness lie? It certainly is not in fashion nor folly. But it surely dwells in the inward bosom of man.

If no peace nor pleasure dwell there,
Tell me, if we'll find it elsewhere.
If in the gay and giddy dance
You should meet smiles, by chance,
Twould only be a mockery of the soul within,
To veil the true feelings of a life of sin.

For the gay trappings of earthly show
Can never make happy a life of woe.
Silks and satins apparently may cover shame,
But the heart within with the pangs of blame
Must suffer on, a fettered prisoner still,
Bound by the unlearned human will.
You have often been told to watch and pray,
But watch as well as work, I say.

For us to be successful in any branch of business or industry we must of a necessity understand it thoroughly. Hence the importance of the culture and development of the brain. For the brain was given to man for a special use, and the more it is cultivated the greater use we can make of it, as the brain is the propelling power of man, and without it he would be nothing more than brute creation—would possess, alike the animals, instinct enough to protect himself. Now we understand that instinct is a natural attribute belonging to man as well as the lower animals. But the intellect is a divine faculty, which alone belongs to man. And I say there is no man (and when I say man, I mean woman, to be sure, as I think she is man's equal in this respect) but what has brain sufficient to make a perfect man of himself, if he would only strive to cultivate it up to its proper standard—have all of its faculties fully developed.

> There is a higher, a nobler life, for us to fill,
> Subject to our own power and will.
> Then let us our progressive elements expand,
> Have them for usefulness always at our command.
> Yes, there is a higher, nobler life for man,
> Beyond this mystic veil's narrow span.

But some one, perhaps, is ready to say that all men and women can't make smart men and women. They can, to the full extent of their brain. My friends, you do not know, you can not realize, the capacity of your brain until it is fully devel_oped. You know not what hidden treasures lie dormant beneath the uncultivated soil of your brain. You know not where nor how much precious gold lies in the bowels of the earth, awaiting development. And the brain of man is a mine of wealth and luxury, a mine of rich thought, awaiting development.

And friends, you certainly are responsible creatures for this neglect of duty you owe to yourselves and to an all-wise Creator, who has entrusted great and precious gifts to your care, that you have neglected and suffered to lie buried underneath the foul and corrupt soil of ignorance and crime, thus falling short of the place and position in life designed for you by your Creator.

And oh ! what fearful consequences must await us in the future for such willful neglect on our part ! Now we all know that people's common excuse is, that we can't all be philosophers, consequently they don't try to be anything save a common tool for the sake of money. If we can't all be philosophers, we can be just what God intended we should be, if we would but use and develop the knowledge he has given us, be that large or small.

Every one has their own individual capacity, and if our mental capacity is small, it is very essential that each and every faculty should be carefully cultivated and developed ; for we have none that we can well afford to lose, then it is wise to make the best use of what we have. And if we are blessed with a large capacity, it is given to us for a special and grand purpose, and we can't well afford to risk such a great responsibility by such willful neglect. Of course some people have a larger capacity than others, which is clearly demonstrated by nature, for we see as many perfect objects in nature of a diminutive form as we do larger ones. So far as nature is concerned, we find as many perfect objects, or men and women of a small stature to be as perfect in their form and respective portion of intellect as the larger ones. Why not? 'Tis just as easy to make most anything as perfect on a small scale as on a larger one. Each and every one have their own portion of intellect, if any at all. I cannot say whether it be large or small.

But be it what it may, let us strive to cultivate it and bring forth each and every faculty to its proper standard. Consequently we will have more perfect men and women, and not so many substitutes. You may frequently hear people say that it

would not be well for society at large to have universal education. Why? Because, they say, there would be too many smart
men and women trying to make a living without work. Now,
my dear friends, this is a sad mistake, as you very well know
that an active brain is not indolent. And you seldom, if ever see
a lazy, indolent man or woman smart, or a smart man or woman
that is lazy. If you think you do, it is only your own mistake. You are only mistaken in the capacity of the individual.
For it is an evident fact that a lazy, indolent person does not
possess an active brain; if they did, they could not be content
in idleness, consequently would not be lazy. 'Tis not culture that
makes people indolent. It is most assuredly for the want of it.
This indolent disposition of people is but their own natural
instinct. Some persons have as their native instinct, industrious
habits. Some have as a natural instinct, thieving, roguish habits;
others the reverse to this. Each and every one have their own
peculiarities in their native instinct. It is not culture that makes
thieves and rogues, but often prevents it. Education and culture
never caused any man or woman to err. But it was their own
native element, their natural instinct was to err. Culture only
enlarges the capacity. Without it they would do as much if not
worse crimes, in ignorance.

You sometimes hear it said that an education makes fools of
some people. This is a mistake, as they were fools in the beginning—t'was not their education made them so. And we had as
well have well-informed fools as illiterate ones, as they are about
as profitable. We need never to be alarmed about our having
too many smart people in the world. Let us have all we can,
the more the better. For people are like the flowers and tender
plants of the earth. Each kind of a flower has its own peculiar
fragrance and beauty. Also the herbal plants have their peculiar
uses in the economy of nature. So each and every individual
possesses his or her own peculiar talent. And the culture and

development of man is similar to the cultivation of plants and flowers. It only makes them more useful and beautiful, without a change of their natural use. As you are well aware that with the finest cultivation in the world, you could not produce a geranium from a poppy plant, neither could you cultivate mustard plants so as to produce cabbage. Certainly not. But with the proper cultivation you could produce a finer flower of its kind, and a more perfect plant of its kind, which would increase its usefulness in the economy of nature.

So with the education of man. You cannot change the color of his skin, neither his original disposition. But with the proper culture you can fit him for a higher, a more noble and useful life—a greater pleasure and benefit to himself and society. Now there is a false idea prevalent among the common classes of people, and that is, they think it only requires an education for literary pursuits. But, my friends, this is a grand mistake· Your minds need to be cultivated and developed, no matter what occupation in life you intend to follow. Because men are educated, that does not necessitate them all to be lawyers, doctors nor statesmen. Far from it. We want educated men and women in each and every avocation in life. Then we will be more successful and enterprising.

We need well-educated men for farmers, mechanics and for all tradesmen, fully as well as for lawyers and other professional men, as there is a science in all professions of life. Farming or agricultural industries is looked upon by a large majority of people as an inferior profession or drudge life. One of the greatest reasons for this is for the want of the proper instructions, of a higher development of the intellectual faculties. Farming is a good profession, if properly followed, and needs as much scientific research as any other branch of business, and should be one of the most independent and self-sustaining professions there is to-day, if men would but try to make it so.

But farmers are like a great many other people whose minds and tastes do not run after a literary life, conclude there is no use of any education, any further than enough to know how to spell, read, and write a little; so they can read the newspapers and write to their friends occasionally. They think they were born farmers, and farmers they must be; and their boys are born farmers, and farmers they must be, whether they want to be or not. And their daughters are educated in about the same way as their sons. They are house-maids, and milk-maids, for they were born in that station of life, and accordingly must stay there. And if they can read and write a little, that is sufficient, as they never expect to go up higher in life, consequently have no need of any more.

This is one among the saddest errors in our land to-day, in the way of intellectual and moral development. To see the hundreds of bright-eyed, intelligent boys and girls growing up into the years of woman and manhood, with their youthful minds stagnated by surrounding influences of commmonalities, as the mind is certainly developing all the while the physical form is maturing. Then how necessary to have early training to cultivate it, and enlarge the reasoning faculties before bad principles are inculcated and pernicious habits are formed, making a revolting barrier to the ingrowing of a better spirit.

You know not what your boys and girls might be, if they had only the opportunity. You know not how many great statesmen might be developed out of a country life, nor how many great women might spring into a world of usefulness and renown from a rural country home. I see no reason why they should not, as the country, so far as nature or natural objects are concerned, is far more favorable for both the moral and intellectual development than city life, as there they are surrounded with more of God's works and less of man's. For what is better calculated to inspire within the mind a more lofty and noble feeling of awe and admiration than to wander along beside a stream, where its clear purling waters is gently flowing down its onward course, shaded by the majestic old oaks, that have perhaps witnessed a century of years, and could, if they had the power of speech, tell many a tragic story and romantic legend of yore, that now stand as a monument of time and strength.

It is not the profession that makes the man, but the man that makes the profession a success. To be successful in any enterprise, we must have the right kind of material to work with. People too often value an invidual for the sake of a title, when really they do not deserve it, and this is an evil that is robbing our country of worthy men and women, as this a strong temptation for the ambitious, restless spirit of the youth to grasp after to secure a name, whether they deserve it or not. When an empty name will fill the place and position in life that one full of merit would, why then (say they) expend so much time and labor for something you can have without. This is the reason that we have so many quacks among our professional people. We should not trust to an individual's outward appearance, but endeavor to find out their true principles. If they be good, value them for their merit; if they are bad, discard them at once. We must learn to discriminate people, to find what their differences are. And in trying—

To find what their principles are,
Judge us not by the dress we are able to wear.
Nay, judge not the person by their dress,
Esteem them for the noble qualities they possess.

Never the gee-gaws of a cox-comb admire,
Never his fair-spoken blandiloquence desire,
In self-respect always civil gentility demand,
Enhance thy charms only by virtue's command.

And now, my dear friends, we should lay aside all foolish notions and technicalities, false pride and prejudice, and look at life as it really is, as something that is real, that is earnest; not an imaginary dream, a floating gossamer on the silvery wings of fancy, only to be shocked by the fearful awakening out of its sweet slumber of ideal bliss into stern realities. We must view life as it is, and look to our everyday surroundings, and see if it is lived practically.

Ah! methinks when thine eyes are lifted up with the hope of seeing, thine heart will sink in sickening disgust at the sight of so many miserable failures and wrecked forms of humanity. Therefore it would be useless for me to tell you, that there is a great and grand work for us to do, as you are not blind in regard to your duty, only indifferent, and that is so much worse on your part, for indifference is a greater evil than blinded ignorance. And, my friends, that feeling of indifference is one of the darkest clouds that hangs over this beautiful land of ours to-day; fully as disastrous to good morals as intemperance.

> For indifference is one of the largest boats
> That on life's broad-bosomed ocean floats,
> Sailing rapidly o'er its turbid waters wild,
> Bearing its cargo of human souls as a wayward child,
> To the homes of misery, want, and woe,
> Robbed of life's chiefest blessings by this vital foe.

O then let us rouse up and shake off this stupor of indifferent slumber, and awaken to a full sense of our duty, and try to save ourselves, our children, our neighbors, and our neighbors' children from a life of immorality, wretchedness, and woe. Let no one excuse themselves by saying that they can't reform the world. Nay, but you can do your part, and that is what no one else can do, as each and every one have their own influence. Words and actions are not meaningless; they have a signification of their own. If 'tis not good, it is certainly evil. Every word we speak does good or harm.

A trifle, a little word not rightly spoken,
May make a friend heart-broken.

Therefore, we should be very careful how we characterize ourselves. Remember, the greatest and grandest objects of life are made up of little deeds, actions, and words. Would you call a man or woman great or noble, who never did but one good deed in their lives? Certainly not.

A man's life is chiefly made up of little deeds; if good in their combination, they make him a great and noble man; if evil, they make him a desperate piece of wrecked humanity, as it is by the combination of small things or particles and unity, that anything of importance is ever completed. For there is nothing in nature that came into existence a complete form. The thousands of shining leaflets which adorn the forest trees were not complete until they grew in nature to be so. Every spire of grass, vine, leaf, and flower, grew little by little, until they became perfect in nature. So it is with all of earth's creatures; they are subject to development.

Now, we understand that development is divided into two distinct classes, natural and artificial, and might be properly sub-divided into four classes, inclusive of moral and spiritual development, and that natural development belongs to all earthly objects as well as living creatures. Artificial development is something acquired above or outside of the natural outgrowth, which may belong to animals as well as man, for we often see animals taught to perform many wonderful feats, which, as a matter of fact, is not their own natural ability. But moral and spiritual development belongs alone to man, and if he neglects to cultivate and expand these higher orders of development, he is not much above the brute creation in the way of enjoyment and usefulness. So, my friends, it is clearly demonstrated, that we can perform life's duties one by one, ultimately making life a great and grand achievement. And for us to excuse ourselves by saying, we can't reform the world. This is just as simple as for a merchant to close his doors and say, because he can't sell all the goods in the city he won't sell any, and a mechanic to lock up his tools · and say, because he could not build all the houses in the city, he would not build any, and the farmer to say, because he could not cultivate all the land in the country, he would not cultivate any, and the doctor to say, because he could not possibly go to see all the sick people in the city, he would not go to see any patient. Then we would be in a fix, and getting fixer every day, as we could buy no goods to wear. Then, I know, the ladies would make a terrible racket. We would soon have no houses to live in, and nothing from the farm to eat, and if we managed to live through these difficulties, and happened to get sick, as we frequently do, we would have to die and end our miserable existence, as we could get no physician to come to our relief, because he could not relieve everybody, he would not relieve any.

> Now, my friends, they say,
> 'Tis a poor rule that works only one way;
> It is a false theory you see,
> For the latter excuses are in every degree,
> As practical as the former ones.

Then let us not excuse ourselves by saying that we can't reform the world. We don't expect you to do it, but you can do your part, and that is something no one else can do, and that is all we ask you to do, is your part, and that would influence some one else to do their part, which, as a natural consequence, would induce others to do their part, and so on, until you would know not where nor how far your influence might extend, nor how many human lives you might save from a total wreck.

Now, we must take the common-sense view of these things,

and value them just for what they are worth, for 'tis this way you know yourselves, that there is no one so low down in life, nor so mean, ignorant, nor indolent, but what have their influence. And if Jim Jenkins should reform, his friend, Bill Smith, would follow suit, as he would think himself as good-looking, smart, and of as good parentage as Jim Jenkins, and if he could reform and make a man of himself, could see no rea on why he should not, And perhaps a half dozen more of the associates would follow the example through the same influence. And if you are an individual of a good moral, influential standing, so much more good you can do, as your influence is so much greater, for it is not confined only among your associates, but runs out in a much larger circle. And you know not to-day how many young men and women you hold in command through your influence. Then, my friends, be careful how you wield that power, for if it be evil and demoralizing, oh! what fearful consequences await you, what dreadful responsibilities to answer for. Then let no one excuse themselves by saying, they can't reform the world. You can help, and your help is as much as any other individual's help of the same capacity, and all of our helps combined will make one grand whole help.

Oh! that people were as deeply interested in moral, mental, and social culture as they are in the getting of wealth. Yea, if they were half as much interested they would find it a comparative easy task to live a higher, a nobler life than they now do. I tell you, my friends, " where there's a will, there's a way " to do most anything. And when we find no way, there's no will to search for it, consequently it is not found. And when I hear people say, they can't do anything. I know they don't try. Their interest is not there, as their incapabilities lie mostly in their disinterestedness.

What is the great aim and object of life? Is it not a struggle for pleasure and happiness? Just let us consider a moment and reflect, as reflection is what we need in this age of the world, and from the word reflection we convey to the mind two or three distinct ideas. First, is a pause, or consideration which is valuable to us, as it often prevents harm through hasty conclusions. Secondly, from reflection an idea of light is thrown upon anything, which is very essential, as we need all the light we can get, and as little darkness as possible. Thirdly, an image thrown back by reflection, which is very useful to us, as it often shows us our ugly actions, when otherwise they might pass unnoticed. Then reflection, in every sense of the word, is what we need in this age. People act too often on a momentary impulse, without mature judgment; hence we see so many miserable lives fraught with wrecked hopes, mocked by the dim shadows of the past. When life's early morn, like the sweet-scented rose, unfolding its tender leaflets, imbibing the genial warmth of the glowing sun, invigorated by the sparkling gems of heaven's dew, was opening into a life of loveliness, in a moment, by one rude blast, lies a wreck of shattered beauty. So in life's early morn, when out on the grand old ocean of time, your life-boat is quietly sailing o'er its gentle and heaving tide, glowing in the transport of momentary happiness, often drifts away from life's more important duties, seemingly unconscious of the stormy clouds of care and danger that constantly threaten to shipwreck your tottering barks of hope, until they are capsized and run aground on the shoals of defeat and disappointment. Ah! 'tis too late then, to pine o'er your lost and ruined hopes. But now is the propitious time, for we can only claim to-day, as to-morrow may never come to us. Then, my friends, let each and every one take hold of life's duties in earnest, and go to work, not for the glory, but for the good we may do. And if we have been negligent in the past, let us make amends for it, by our faithfulness in the future. Let our precepts be such that no reproach can follow in their footsteps, as our advice and admonition to the young will avail nothing, if our precepts are not worthy of example. And when we advise the young people to shun certain vices, we must not indulge in them ourselves. And if we teach them to be careful of their associations, to have no companionship with immoral persons, we must of necessity discountenance all such ourselves. Pass their crimes by with no degree of allowance, neither for pity's sake, nor any other sake, as the young must have examples either to profit by or follow. We must have a beginning and a stopping place somewhere, and the sooner the better, else the world will go to ruin.

Some people, for the sake of financial interest, pass by the greatest crimes of immorality unnoticed, when otherwise it would be to them a perfect horror. But the almighty dollar will cover a mountain of sins from the eyes of this world. Now, my dear friends, this is an evil that is bringing down its thousands of young people into the " cess-pool of crime " and degradation, as they say your example and precept teaches them that money makes people respected with neither principle nor good morals. We must disown and discountenance immorality for the crime itself, in whatever form it comes. Neither respect it for its money, nor disrespect it on account of its poverty, but the crime itself should be condemned by all good moral people, no matter what form it comes to you in. Let us take the common-sense view of life and make it practical, and lay aside those foolish notions and prejudices in regard to a man or woman's occupation or position in life, making them a superior or inferior being to that of his fellow-creatures.

Let us look at a man or woman's principle and intelligence as a more important and worthy attainment than wealth or fine dress, for what is more disgusting to a sensible man or woman than to see a mass of ignorance wrapped up in fine goods. Intelligence lends an air of grace to an individual,—gives them a noble appearance that cannot be mistaken for check, as check is

14

the offspring of ignorance, and is disgusting in any place you find it, and the fore-runner of premature thought. Precept and example are the two great controlling powers of the moral universe. They must either save the world, or sink it down into the lowest depths of degradation and crime. If you doubt this assertion, just look around you in every-day life, and see the hundreds of people who profess to be good, moral, and even some of them Christian people, who by precept and example you could not distinguish them from the common class of immoral ones. Then is is it any wonder that crime and immorality has such a terrific reign in our country? 'Tis not a strange phenomena to any close observer, one who reflects, as they see incidents of this kind occurring every day, recognized by the general public. There are a great many false notions, nowadays, prevalent among the people, and we should try to search them out and locate them, as people often err in trying, as they think, to do right. This is for the want of investigation, for we should never do anything without a reason or motive, and be sure it is a good one. Individuals so often act on the impulse of the moment, and, unless they are well disciplined, nine times out of ten they do wrong on such occasions. You must investigate, you must train your mind to know right from wrong, and when you meet with either one of the gentlemen, Mr. Right or Mr. Wrong, you will not be mistaken, but you will know exactly how to salute him. But some people think it a Christian duty, or feeling, to be what they call sociable with every one they meet, but, my friends, this is a false position to hold, as we are commanded not to keep company, neither to bid Godspeed to an evil-doer; if so, we are partakers of their evil deeds. If an individual is guilty of any crime, or immoral conduct that we hold ourselves above doing, they have no right to claim recognition from us. And when we recognize such an individual socially, we commit an error against ourselves and families, and the public good morals, because our influence for good among the youth is lost, as they would say, "you don't practice what you teach." And because we have business transactions with individuals does not compel us to associate with them, neither to recognize them in society, outside of a business affair. And if every one would act con scientiously in this matter, regardless of the few nickels and dimes they might lose from this class of persons, they would soon see quite a revolution in society circles, as this low class of immoral people would soon learn that decent and respectable individuals would not notice them an further than business compelled them to do. Consequently this would be a very forcible example for the young to profit by, as they would dread the very idea of being discarded and abandoned by all of the respectable class of society. Hence, you see the propriety of precept and example. If otherwise than this, the young people say, in their reasoning: "What does it matter how I conduct myself, or whether I have a good reputation or not, as it is not a man's character that makes people respect him and recognize him in society, but his money and fine apparel; so the money and fine clothes I must have, get it any way I can—it is about the same; so I get it, that is all that is necessary, as it will give me friends, character and a position in life." But, my friends, it ought to be a very low position. For what is money worth to an individual without any moral standing? Not anything, further than to satisfy a morbid appetite and a temporary gratification of lustful desires. And when this is said, all is said in the way of a benefit.

As filthy lucre can never satisfy the soul,
For its inward craving of glittering gold
Is to purchase both happiness and health,
Fully as much as honor and wealth.
To be defeated in its chief object and aim,
Would be a life of woe, lived in vain.

For wealth cannot quiet the conscience within
Of a life of suffering, shame and sin.
No visitation of disaster incidental to human life
Embraces so vast a realm in misery and strife
As the deviation from moral rectitude into the disgrace
Of immoral shame, which hides her blushing face,
And mantles her brow with a dismal cloud,
To veil the inward feeling of thoughts so loud
That perchance they might unawares betray
A life of reproach, contempt and dismay.
Remember, our lives are what we make them,
That for good or evil our friends must take them.

Then, it is of the utmost consequence that strict discipline
should accompany our every-day walks of life, that we throw no
shadows in the beautiful, bright pathway of the youth. As we
are the advanced guard, only a few years ahead of them, instead
of leaving stumbling stones for them to fall over, let us remove
them, as this is our duty.

And the great responsibilities for them let us feel,
"As life is earnest, and life is real."
Let our precepts and examples always be
For the young, life's sequel undisguised and free,
As there's no inspiration of the enlightened soul
That is so great, and grand, in life's control,
As those hallowed influences, imparting new grace,
Giving hope and strength to a down-fallen race
Of the power of erring man to reform and redeem
A degraded life to the favor of moral esteem,
And as days, months and years roll on,
May we see the returning of a mighty throng
From the wayward paths of folly and crime,
To a life of usefulness, more deserving and sublime.

My friends, there is, perhaps, a great deal more of importance attached to precept and example than many of you are
aware of. It undoubtedly wields a greater influence over the youthful mind than instruction, as we see the youth who has been reared
in the country, and lived a rustic life, as a general rule possess
better morals, with a greater development of their natural
powers, than those who have been reared and educated in the
glow and glitter of city life. As children who have been accus
tomed to city life from infancy, their youthful minds are mostly
developed by precept and example, for the sense of sight to the
external organs is far more impressive on the youthful mind
than instruction is to the eyes of the understanding. Hence you
see the power of precept and example, as you could not doubt
for a moment but that the city mothers love their dear little boys
as fondly as a country woman, and take as much pains to teach
them the right way to honor and usefulness, and to shun the evil
ways of life, that inevitably bring destruction to those that
practice them.

But look a moment, if you please, over your city, and see
whether those boys and girls follow their mother's instructions,
or the precepts and examples they have before them every day.
I will leave this for the public morals of your surroundings to
decide, as that will be more conclusive and convincing to your
mind.

And you are well aware that some of our greatest men and
woman have sprung from a country life. Why? Because they
had good instruction in early youth at home, when the mind was
unencumbered with the cares of the world, and was susceptible
of early impressions, which are lasting. And the precepts and
examples were appropriate to the occasion, thereby giving point
and force to the instruction they had received, thereby gaining a
more ready access both to their understandings and hearts-
Hence it must be conclusive to any unbiased mind that instruc.

tion is not worth anything unless followed by the right kind of
precept and example, as most any individual could, from the
right sense of feeling and sympathy, give good advice, but oh !
so few have the moral courage to face the world in right, and set
the proper precepts and examples which are to reform mankind,
if it should happen to be deleterious to their financial affairs, as
that almighty dollar is too precious to be lost, if it sinks the
world in degradation.

And oh ! my friends, have you never thought over this matter
seriously. If not, just pause a moment, and when you fully
realize the true import of your actions in regard to your financial
affairs, as being of a greater importance than the kind of precepts
and examples that you give to your children for an inheritance,
you will see that you are then setting a price upon their lives and
future prosperity. And this very thought should be one of awe
and astonishment to every thinking man and woman, for there
are none of us excused from the duties we owe to ourselves and
our fellow-creatures. No matter what avocation in life we follow,
we are all alike responsible. We are responsible for the higher
development of our intellectual faculties, it matters not where
we live nor what our occupation is. If in the bustling city or in
the quiet country home, we need the higher development of the
living principles of the mind.

And we need educated women in every avocation of life, fully
as much as men, for they have an important work to do in the
great drama of life. But, I'm sorry to say, there is a false idea
among a goodly number of ladies, like it is with some men—
they think it is of no consequence whether they are educated or
not, any further than to read and write a little (so they may read
their husband's love letters, if he gets any, as some of them do,
frequently to their shame) unless they intend to follow a literary
life. But, my dear lady friends, this is a false theory, for an
education and a cultured mind fits women for a higher and

nobler life, qualifies them for a greater usefulness, as it makes them better wives, better house-keepers, better mothers, and more pleasant companions for their friends. Just think, what is more pleasing than to meet with an intelligent, well-cultured lady, who possesses a noble, affable disposition? For such ladies you always find highly entertaining and instructive, courteous and polite, especially to strangers.

For ignorance is self-conceited, proud, arogant and puffed up with bigotry. And when in public assemblies, if you will note those who curl the lips with scorn, and sneer at those whom they think are not so well dressed as themselves, you will find that they are those who have by accident come into possession of a little money, and being burdened with their ignorance, try to put on unnecessary style, as this is their only resource. As they have more style than brains, then of course it comes first. Never in my life have I envied this class of people, but God knows my heart has always pitied them for their ignorance.

There is none but what have their weakness.
For such we should, in the spirit of meekness,
Reprove their faults and pity their delusion,
As it is in vanity they are given this illusion.
Then in a higher, a nobler sense of duty,
Let us view life in all her primeval beauty,
When the stars sang together for joy,
When peace and good will without alloy,
To man on this beautiful earth was given,
To make his home an earthly heaven.
But ah ! wayward man, tell me not
That fate decreed your unhappy lot.
'Tis your cowardly weakness that is overcome
By the tempter, when the victory is won.

But, my friends, you know full well "that 'tis human both to

err" and to excuse, as people never do anything but what they
can find some excuse for doing it—

> If 'tis next to nothing ; a poor one,
> They say, 'tis better than none,
> For the highway wickedness of to-day
> Has among multitudes of people its way.
> And oh ! my dear friends, how long
> Shall this be said of a mighty throng,
> Who, underneath their unhallowed feet
> Morally desecrates our liberties so sweet,
> Be allowed unchained and unfettered free,
> To lock up virtue with an immoral key,
> Shadowing the hopes of our sons and daughters?
> Methinks I hear an echo, come across the waters :
> Oh ! how long shall this dark, dismal cloud
> Our loved ones and loved homes enshroud ?

> Is there no one who will devise a plan,
> Open up the way, and lead the van ;
> That will rally the forces of glorions right,
> No matter how long nor hard the fight,
> To drive away the gloomy clouds of to-day
> Which darken our skies with sad dismay ;
> Ere vice and crime for our hopeful morrow
> May add to our hearts a new sad sorrow ?

> Then let us lay aside all foolish pride,
> And march on to victory with a gigantic stride—
> Heed not the stormy clouds which lower,
> And the shadows that gather around our door ;
> But look onward and upward with hope,
> For in life's ever-changing, uncertain scope,
> We see in the distance a beautiful star,
> Beaming brightly in the future afar.

Oh ! bright and beautiful star of hope,
We see thee as a spark at a distance remote.
We hail thee, in thy glorious form,
Beckoning to us in life's fearful storm.
And though the night be ever so dark,
With hope in the palpitating heart,
Blazing up in the despair-frozen bosom,
Repletes our soul with an inward heaven.

'Tis hope, you bright little star which we see in yon dark-curtained future, amidst the murky clouds of despair, which seems but a pale, glimmering spark afar, almost quenched by the unceasing showers of melting tears, poured from the dismal clouds of grief and care. But whilst we are rapidly drifting down time's herculean stream, drawing nearer to the hidden realms of and the lamp of life is fast waning, it begins to brighten eternity, as the life-giving rays of hope beams with a crystaline light over the shrouded vale which hangs between us and the morrow ;

As in youth, so when thy locks are thin and hoary,
It still reigns in the bosom with all its glory.

Then, my friends, if we have neglected life's duties, and though we are in the sear and yellow leaf, let not the declining years be an obstruction to the good we may yet do, as we are living examples to the young, and past experience has taught us a lesson that we should not soon forget, as we can now look back on life's bewildering track and see the many precious opportunities which we have so wilfully neglected, and sensibly realize their loss. For we feel the great burden of responsibility rests on the parents and guardians of this age, for the great immorality that now exists; for this vile cloud of licentiousness and dissipation has not just sprung up into existence, but has been gradually rising and accumulating for a number of years, and through our negligence and indifference has assumed its present fearful magnitude. And whilst a goodly number of us have not acquiesed in these evils, yet we have recognized them in not having noticed and condemned their evil practices. We have acted on the principle of taking care of ourselves and allowing other people the same privilege ; and in so doing we have allowed evil influences to grow up among our children, to contaminate their minds with corrupt principles.

Then, in order to protect ourselves and their future welfare, we are, of a necessity, compelled to take active and energetic measures to awaken the people to a full sense of their duties ; as they have, through, indifference, fallen into a deep slumber, and are unconscious of the dangers that are hovering around them. And when once fully awakened to a complete realization of the great power and influence of immorality which is thrown around the youths of to-day, methinks every pure-minded moral man and woman will bravely step into the ranks, and by their actions say, "Here am I, ready to battle for right, which will no one wrong."

My friends, I tell you the time has come for us not only to talk, but to act. We must take a decisive stand either for or against immorality. A line of demarkation must be drawn in society circles. We must let our actions decide whether or not we are for reformation and good morals. We must try to rescue as many of the fallen race as we possibly can, and try to save others from a like disgrace.

This is an age of progress in arts, in scientific research, and discoveries, and why not improve the morals and higher life of man, that is, his intellectual developement? The standard in which society has arrived to, at the present day, no lady or gentleman's social standing is safe. They are liable to be assailed and ruined any day by malicious tongues. For how often do you hear men say, they don't believe there is scarcely any woman but what could be induced to step aside faom the paths of virtue.

O ! what a shame for a man to say this. Remember, young man, if you have no sisters you all have a mother, whether she is an earthly pilgrim or a heavenly saint, I know not. But be that as it may, how would you like to hear such intimations about her? Methinks that it would not be very palatable. O, I know how some men look at this. They say they have seen so many do thus and so, that their confidence in woman is shaken. But how is it on the other hand? Have the women no cause to lose confidence in man? Do not men deceive women? Nine cases out of ten man is the instigator of woman's wrongs; the records will prove this. "Woman is as false as she is fair," is a proverb among the young men of to-day. Why? Because so many poor, untaught and misguided girls have been persuaded by profligate, immoral young men to step aside from the moral paths of rectitude into a life of shame and disgrace., their beauty having proved a snare to their soul. So, young ladies, beware when a man praises your beauty; be sure it is for no good, for when the eyes are ravished with beauty the mind is liable to err.

When we see society so demoralized and depraved as to look upon every stranger that comes into a community or city with a suspicious eye, 'tis a sad, sad thing, indeed.

In view of the foregoing facts, with the most degrading forms of immorality which prevail in all of our large cities at the present day, it is an evident fact that the time has arrived in which all good citizens who feel an interest in the common weal of our country, in order to protect and secure good morals among the youth, should take active measures at once to counteract those evil influences, to retard their onward progress by uniting themselves into reform societies where they can meet together, and establish a code of laws, rules and regulations to govern its members, in connection with a literary department for the encouragement of home literature among the youth at large, as

the nation's future prosperity depends largely on the morals of
its people and their intellectual power.

We know 'tis common to hear people say they don't believe
in secret societies. That little word, secret, is a terror to many
people's minds. They are by that bugbear, like they are by a
good many others, they are frightened when there's none to be
found. They do not consider that we must enjoin secrecy in a
certain part of an order's workings to secure protection from
imposition from outside parties, and enable us to recognize each
other without the knowledge of others. People say a great
many things without due consideration. We must not rely
altogether on what people say, but investigate for ourselves, as
people's say doesn't amount to much every time.

Just take a perspective view of men's public affairs of to-day,
and see what means they have to resort to for protection, in the
way of organizations. For instance, we have the Knights of
Labor, the Farmers' Alliance, and the United Brotherhood,
besides a dozen of others that might be mentioned, organized for
the purpose of protection against other organized bodies. And
if people organize into societies to protect their financial interests, why object to reform societies, as they protect both
personal and financial interests. As the world grows wiser, we
need more wisdom and precaution to carry us through it successfully, for we have the wiles of the devil and the wickedness in
highway places to contend with.

Some object to organizations on the plea that a man can form
a resolution and live up to it just as well outside of a society as in
one. But how often is it they do these things? Not one time
out of twenty. Resolutions are very easily made, but very
hard to keep by a large majority of people, unless they are
restrained.

Some will say, I don't believe in secret orders. Why?
Because I never saw much good in them. And perhaps, my

friend, you are one among the many fault-finders, who never find much good in anything that does not exactly harmonize with your feelings. My friend, you must remember that other people have a right to know something as well as yourself, and are just as likely to be right as you are. Before you make a decision you must look to cause and effect, and whatever has a tendency to benefit the greatest number of people is good. And if we can organize reform societies to reclaim the thoughtless, wayward youth, and a place people can look to for aid and protection from the degrading influences of immoral vices, which surround them in every day life, and be a restraint for the unsuspecting youth in the hours of temptation. Why? Is it not a good thing?

You need not tell me it is no restraint to belong to an order of this kind, as reason teaches us better than this; for we all know that a young man is more apt to succumb to temptation when he thinks that he is violating no pledge, and is under no obligation to any one. He feels just like he is free to do as he pleases—'tis no one's business—and that he will just do it this one time, and won't any more. So in this way young people are led on step by step into ruin, when if they had been restrained by their honor and reputation they might have been saved.

And where there is one that violates their pledge and sacrifices their honor, there are two who do not, in these reform societies. And this should stimulate us to work.

Now, my friends, if there ever was a time in the history of your lives when your work was needed, it is undoubtedly now, for the harvest is great and ready to be reaped, and the laborers are few. There is no sane man or woman of any age or experience but what will favor good moral precepts and examples, whether they practice them or not. Then we want your influence in this grand work before us. Many of you have sons and daughters who are daily exposed to the most degrading forms of society. Will you not try to arrest this debauchery and crime, which seems to fill the very air we breathe with its obnoxious poison, or will you allow this great privilege to pass unheeded? Oh! be careful how you act, as this is a matter of great importance to you, my dear friends. Perhaps you may not realize it just now, as people often realize their duties when it is too late. But God forbid that in after years you may realize it to your sorrow, the neglect of duty to your children. "For how often do we see fond parent's hearts wrung with bitter anguish; sorrowing their gray hairs are brought down to a premature grave." For what? For a lost and ruined son or daughter, when perhaps their future prospects were as bright and promising as yours are to-day, when the demon overtook and decoyed them into his satanic dens of vice, where they are now lost and ruined, just for the want of timely precept and examples from those in whom they had confidence and looked to for protection. But may the all-seeing eye of our Heavenly Father, who knoweth the ways and means of all men, so direct your minds and hearts that you may never have cause for remorse in this your action of duty.

Then while the day-star of hope brightly beams in our bosom, and the future prospects of our children unclouded by the deeds of darkness, let us put our heads together and work for the good of each other—put our shoulders to the great wheel of reformation and keep it rolling until it makes a grand and complete revolution in society. For it has arrived to an awful crisis; it is fearful to any reflecting mind to look ahead in the future, for the rising generation, unless something is done to remedy these degrading influences of immoral conduct, and elevate the minds of the youth by teaching them to control and subdue their animal passions, and cultivate their intellectual capacities more, as the higher development we have of the intellect, the less animal organism we possess, consequently we would have a higher and better class of morals among our people, as it is the ascendency of animal organism that leads people astray. 'Tis not their ignorance of the evils there is in these practices. It almost seems now that the demon of all kinds of crime is foot-loose. that he is omnipresent, that people surely breathe the poisonous effects out of the very atmosphere which surrounds them, so demoralizing is his influence on society all over the country. 'Tis not an isolated case, here and there, once in awhile, among the young people, who are liable sometimes thoughtlessly to be led into an error, but it is indiscriminate, for about as many of the married people are guilty of treachery and criminal conduct as the younger ones.

What a shame this ought to be to all intelligent people. These facts are developed every day in our immediate vicinity. Husbands and wives are quarreling and separating ; perhaps a husband in a fit of jealousy kills his wife and then commits suicide ; perhaps a wife has been deceived, and, heart-broken, puts an end to her miserable existence by suicide, or perhaps she elopes with another woman's husband, who abandons his wife and children and goes off with his neighbor's wife. Why, this state of affairs is loathsome and disgusting to all pure-minded people, and is ridiculous in an enlightened nation, as ours is to-day. It is worse than the heathens, for what they do is in ignorance, and deserves pity rather than censure.

Now all these evils arise from deception, the effects of bad associations. Let the world grow wiser and better, not wiser and worse. I feel like the good people of our country are beginning to realize the necessity for a change in the public morals of our people, to the advancement of our future welfare and prosperity as a civilized and enlightened nation, and are try-ing to reach the means through the temperance cause. But I fear their arms will prove too short, unless they have the proper auxilliaries. We must teach people right from wrong before we can force them to a conclusion, and to punish a lot of violators we must not encroach on the liberty of others.

As for temperance, I have practiced it strictly all of my life because I believed it right. I am an advocate of temperance in all things, more especially whisky. Yet I think that immorality has fully as great a demand on our attention as intemperance, for the temperance cause has been ably discussed for the last twenty years, and has accomplished but little in the way of social morals. It needs appropriate auxilliaries to encourage and stimulate the young, to show them the beauties and benefits arising from good morals, and the evils arising from intemperance, and to restrain those who are not habituated to strong drink from encouraging the popular sentiment of its use by not joining temperance societies, as they claim the pledge enjoined by temperance societies is not temperance, but strict prohibition, and debars them of their rights and liberties as American citizens, for which many, many men would rather die than to sacrifice.

Then let us not bring up the temperance cause as a political issue, but a question of morals. And in this grand moral association, we do not ask them to make a surrender of their rights and privileges as free American citizens, only their duties which they owe to themselves and families in helping to restore society to a state of good morals.

Then, my friends, let us lay aside all foolish pride, and divest ourselves of all party prejudice, and join in one of the noblest schemes of modern invention, in the moral and intellectual development of the higher life of man. As our world certainly grows wiser, let us help to make it grow better, as this is our precious privilege of to-day. For we have a great and grand government, one of the grandest republics in the world of free institutions. Then let us enjoy its glorious privileges, while we guard well its tree of liberty, as it flourisheth like a green bay

tree ; its boughs are reaching far out and upward into the beautiful horizon of the future, and its glorious renown is envied by
all the nations of the earth. Then; whilst we are sweetly reposing underneath its cooling shades, sheltered from the scorching
heat of tyranny and anarchy, in grateful remembrance and
appreciation of the trials and struggles of our forefathers, the
founders of our grand republic and noble institutions, to purchase these precious liberties that we so lavishly enjoy, to make
a great and noble people of their posterity. Then let us not
retrograde, fall short of life's grand purposes, thereby defeating
the greatest objects and aims of their hopes and life struggles,
and though their bodies lie inclosed in the silent tomb, yet our
actions should demonstrate to the world that their minds and
noble deeds still live in the hearts and memories of their
descendants.

So let us, with eager grasp,
Seize each moment as they pass,
To accomplish some good in life's task,
For mankind in each and every class.

WISDOM.

Wisdom, that has long lain wrapped in mystery, is now
gently unfolding her ample robes on the wings of time, spread-
ing her genial rays of light on the dark vale of future years.
Like the dawning of the sun on a dreary day, all around us
seems dark and gloomy, rayless and cheerless ; but presently the
blazing sun dazzles with his melting beams, dispels the hazy fog,
and, as the mist slowly rolls away, it grows brighter and brighter
until the lambent flame is universally spread throughout hill and
dale.

15

Filling our joyless hearts with happy sunshine,
Driving dull care from our wearied minds,
Confirms our hopes, elevates our joys,
Relieves our sighs and our fear destroys—

Making a fine display of the arbitrary powers of Deity, thereby showing us how soon the dark shades of misfortune can vanish. So wisdom unfolds her gigantic pages one by one, diffusing light into the dark cavities of superstitious ignorance, renovating society to a higher state of refinement, until finally it will expand throughout the whole universe, which doubtless was intended from the beginning of creation, as we have fair illustrations of the fact through the divine agency of an all-wise providence. For if we will notice closely the works of nature, we will find that everything is formed with profound wisdom, even from the smallest pebbles to the huge mountains, the least rivulet to the largest river. In the first formation of a mountain, we readily understand, begins its outgrowth from the minute pebbles and small grains of sand in accumulating with each other, gradually growing for a number of years, ultimately forms a gigantic mountain. And likewise the small rivulets flowing together, and depositing their small streams of water in the low flats, which in flowing off forms branches and creeks, thus soon produce large rivers, lakes, gulfs and oceans.

And when we take their general properties and uses of their different formations, we find some very fine illustrations. The mountains, though they seem so unsuited for the residence of man, yet they have their uses in the economy of nature. They accumulate the moisture, thereby producing clouds, which send down cool and refreshing rains on the parched and thirsty earth, gently reviving all nature. And the rivers, though so ill-shaped, have their uses in the economy of nature. Their windings greatly augment their utility by affording facilities for a more extended intercommunication, and prevents such velocity of

current as would otherwise in many streams prevent them from
being bridged or navigated in safety.

Thus we see wisdom unfolds her ample pages,
Disclosing the priceless treasures of hidden ages
To the ever-searching inquiries of man,
Enabling him to complete the most difficult plan.

THE GOLDEN LEAVES.

"It has been so long, I can scarcely remember that I have
ever been a bud," said the leaf in a whisper to its companions;
"but from surrounding circumstances it certainly is an evident
fact that I have been at one time, but it is so far back in the
distance that my memory has failed to keep an account of it.   I
can only sensibly realize my present condition.   I know that I
am now looked upon and esteemed by my fellows for my beautiful golden colors, and can't realize that one attired in such magnificent array ever sprang from such an insignificant thing as a
bud, yet I am told by my green fellows that I once was as green
as they.   But such a thing seems incredible to my mind.   I feel
as though they must be laboring under a mistake.   Then again,
I discover day by day, they begin to brighten and assume a
more comely appearance, until some fellows that I have known
ever since I can distinctly remember, who were once pretty green,
are now able to present a very respectable appearance, and may
possibly at some future time, with the grand advantages they
have in their immediate surroundings of intelligence and noble
examples furnished them by their superiors, acquire a respectable
distinction among their companions.   Yet we should not tolerate
such an opinion within their reach, for fear they should be foolish enough, stimulated with the idea of self aggrandisement,

attempt to ascend the ladder of modern improvement, and with the beneficial experience they have undergone in the past decade, might in all probability be enabled to maintain a more exalted position in the great arena of vegetable existence than ourselves, as you are well aware this is an age of progress, and as the wheels of time revolve around our leafy kingdom, changes are continually presenting themselves, and we should ever be on the alert, as we are well aware that our contemporaries are gaining strength, for we, more or less, feel a trembling and a weakness every time the wind rustles in our midst."

Presently a gentle gale passed through them, and a general twitter set up between them, whereupon a very large golden leaf who occupied a prominent position among the leaves, complacently called attention of his fellow-companions, and in a significant manner said: "My friends, you see from the past rebuke, we have triumphantly maintained our exalted eminence without sbstaining any perceptible loss ; therefore let us take courage from this demonstration of our power, for we have yet the reins of government ; let us run it to suit ourselves, regardless of the dictation of any one, especially those green fellows who, in their ignorance of the grand glories of the golden leaves, could never enjoy such supreme power, for they have neither the brains nor ability to govern so grand a kingdom as this successfully ; and to succumb to their power would certainly be detrimental to both parties, and would annihilate the greatness of this leafy universe."

No sooner than he finished his speech, a heavy gale set up which brought down every golden leaf in dismay to the ground. Being so stunned by the unexpected blow, it was quite a while before anything more was heard from the fallen leaves, whose bright colors soon began to assume sombre shades, instead of their beautiful hues of yellow and gold, when, one lovely October evening a whirlwind began to rustle them around, whereupon one old, dark, crusty leaf, who had in the wind soared up among his rival companions said : "I guess you will be able to run your government very well.   It does not matter much any way to us, for we have had our day and enjoyed it, and as we have about our race run, we can surely, what little time is allotted us in the future, bear what you have, for lo! these many years.   But you certainly can profit by our example ; take care lest when ye think you have all the glory to yourselves, that it does not suddenly depart when least expected."

Upon saying this he whirled around a few times and fell quietly to the ground, where he was numbered with his lost companions.

LADIES AND GENTLEMEN :   As I have been requested by the committee to have something for your kind consideration to-night, I have concluded to make an attempt, and though it be but a feeble one I trust in your generous feeling that you will make due allowance for imperfections.   And I hope if I should speak plain in giving you my sentiments that you take no offense, as my motto is—

> Both to the aged and the youth
> Be sure to always speak the truth ;
> No matter how much, nor what you say,
> Hurt any, or whom it may,
> Be sure your promise to fill, -
> Please any, or whom it will.

And if I should unthoughtedly tresspass on your patience too long, I hope you will excuse me on the rule of a friend's infirmities to bear.   For if, like myself, you possess but a very moderate supply of that material—consequently it is easily exhausted.   However, I shall be brief as possible and only give a few pointed views on the use and abuse of the liquor traffic,

carried on as it is at this day and time.   Now we all know that
ladies, to a certain extent, are by one class of individuals condemned for speaking their sentiments in public.   And I must
say we are too often misrepresented by our bigoted opponent
because we do vindicate our rights in public.   And why not?
Are we slaves?   Have we no rights or privileges, save in the
kitchen and over the wash-tub?   Are we not free American
citizens?   If we are denied the right and privilege of voting to
make laws under which we have to live and abide by, then why
not let us express our sentiments in public without the taunts,
jeers and ridicule of publicmen.   As we are not allowed to act and
our influence is all we have; then if it be good why not let us in any
and all places wield it.   I do not believe it is proper nor fit for a
woman to aspire to public offices, neither do I think it would be
proper for her to go to the polls and vote.   That, I think, would
be out of her place of business.   But I do think woman has the
same right as a man (whether it is allowed or not) to speak her
sentiments in public.   Why not?   You say that woman wields
an influence over man.   Why not let her power be felt in the
public halls as well as in the private home, if it be good?   For
doubtless it would not be out of place, as our public men need
all the good influences that can possibly be thrown around them,
to shield and direct them in the discharge of the sacred duties
entrusted to their care and supervision for the good of the great
masses of our commonwealth.   And if a woman's influence is
good at home and in private circles, it is good in public places
as well.   What it may accomplish is altogether owing to the
manner and direction in which it is used.   But I shall venture
to say, in behalf of the good women of this city, if their true
sentiments were publicly known and properly felt, there would
soon be a radical change in some men's business here, and the
days of these saloons and other public nuisances would be numbered.   No, but the fond mothers and broken-hearted wives

must let their tears fall in silence, and their hearts burst in stifled sobs of care-worn grief over drunken husbands and sons. Why? Because the wives and mothers are women, and it would be out of their place to say anything in public. And it is a God's pity that more of them were not out of the way a little oftener, in this respect, and let their influence be felt abroad, as it certainly is not at home. If it done no other good it would be a timely warning to the young ladies to beware, lest they might unhappily be caught in the same snare. The only safe plan is to remove the temptation from our midst. And until that is accomplished, young men, take a friend's advice—

One who wishes you well :
Shun a dram-shop or whisky house
As you would the gates of hell ;
For to meet him you would be more
Apt than at your mother's door.

You have doubtless been told not to listen to the advice of women ; if you did you would repent it, as the evil spirit was first in woman, and she deceived man. Admit this assertion. But the same authority says that woman was deceived by the Devil or Tempter ; that HE was the most subtle beast of the field. So you can see the point at once. The Evil One is always represented by either one or the other of the two pronouns, " he " or " it ", and we all know that a pronoun is used instead of the noun itself. Now I think this clearly defines the gender of the Evil One. It is true that Mother Eve was de-ceived, but she was deceived by the same kind of a devil that hundreds of other good women are these days, of the masculine gender to be sure. And whenever you see woman that has fallen into disgrace and shame, when it is fully investigated, you will most assuredly find the author of their crime of the same gender. All gentlemen of any intelligence will admit that woman was God's last and best creation. This is why so much more is expected of woman than of man. If she steps aside from the paths of virtue her destiny is doomed. No more will she be respected by the better class of people, which is just and right. But, on the other hand, let a man be guilty of the same crime and people hardly seem to notice it. Why? Because we don't expect much better of men, in one sense of the word. If a woman should get drunk, what a terrible thing! If a man gets drunk, whips his wife twice a week, give the salooon his money, and raise his children in ignorance, this is all right; he is a free American citizen; that is his personal liberty whic he boasts of so much.

Poor women, they must submit to these wrongs. Why? Because they are imposed on them by men, who claim to be the lords of creation, who claim they have the right to make laws to govern women as well as themselves. They claim their laws are founded on justice and the Bible. If so, why not, you gentlemen, the lords of creation, who have it now it your power, give us a law by your boasted rights, to protect our happiness, homes and firesides. And gentlemen, you claim that you enact laws conducive to woman's happiness. If so, prove what you say by your actions in this contest for right, which will wrong no one. Remember, young men, the Bible says (2d chapter Habakak, 15th verse): "Woe unto him that giveth his neighbor drink, that putteth the bottle to him and maketh him drunk," and every man who votes for the liquor traffic is putting the bottle to his neighbor, to our sons and husbands. For what is the difference between the act of those who sell and those who vote for them to sell? One party is just as innocent of crime as the other, as they only do what you by your votes give them a right to do, consequently you are morally responsible for all the evils arising therefrom. Remember the Proverb, (chapter 16, verse 25), "There is a way that seemeth right unto a man, but the end thereof are the ways of death." It may seem right to you to force this liquor traffic on us, but perhaps in the end you may sadly realize your error—

When life's dark shadows around you fall,
And fond remembrance to your minds recall
The untimely end of some loved friend,
Whose life was plucked by the foul fiend—

Who is now using all of his subtle arts, young man, to catch you unawares in his trap. You may be sure that he will be very zealous, will spare no pains if there is the faintest shadow of a hope to secure you. Did you know, my friends, that the devil preached his sermons from the very same Bible that our ministers do? Now just think of it, and if you have never took notice of it, hereafter just watch him and you will see him, every time, take his text either on or in the Bible or about it. He will be sure not to overlook it. He will try to prove to you his arguments from it, and to make his points out of the Bible, when he disbelieves every word of it. But his strong foothold lies in your faith in the scriptures. He knows just how to select out those passages of scripture to suit his own purposes and the misguided views of men. When he makes you believe, he has made his points.

And now, young man, are you willing to sit and fold your arms and let such an one read for you? Are you willing to have him teach you? Are you ready to act on his advice? Nay? consider well; read for yourselves; act for yourselves, as you alone are responsible to God for your actions. Would to God I could and had the time to read to you young men all the places in the holy oracles where wine drinking and strong drink are condemned. But time and space forbids it to-night. I shall only give you a few passages of scripture our honorable opponent is always careful to leave out. Proverbs, 23d chapter, 29th

verse, says : "Who hath woe? who hath sorrow? who hath contentions? who hath babbling? who hath wounds without a
cause? who hath red eyes? They that tarry long at wine. They
that go to seek mixed wine. Look not thou upon the wine when
it is red, when it giveth its color in the cup, when it moveth
aright. At last it biteth like a serpent and stingeth like an
adder." Solomon says, 20th chapter, 1st verse : Wine is a
mocker and strong drink is raging, and whosoever is deceived
thereby is not wise. I think this is sufficient to prove to any
reasonable unbiased mind the evil effects of whisky, that it
causes men to despise the sons of God, causes them to profane
his holy name. And, gentlemen, I will now tell you what I
have heard, and what I never heard, and I don't believe any one
else ever did. I have heard men when under the influence of
whisky curse God, curse Jesus Christ and even curse their own
soul. But never in my life have I heard whisky praise God.
Neither have I heard it curse the devil. Nay, it could not curse
its father, for so long as a child is under the influence of its
parent, of course it would not curse him.

I will close by quoting you one other passage of scripture,
Isaiah, 28th chapter, 7th verse : But they have also erred
through wine, and through strong drink are out of the way.
The priest and prophet have erred through strong drink. They
are swallowed up of wine. They are out of the way through
strong drink. They err in vision, they stumble in judgment.

We are told that death lurks in every flower.
In the deadly conflict dram-drinking is the power
That slyly decoys, and finally destroys,
The greatest number of our friends, husbands and boys.
To the battle he takes our sword with him to fight—
'Tis the Bible, our hope and our light.

For he is very smart, he knows how to play his part,

Just when and where to drive his cart.
I hope when he turns the corner and up the street,
He will not find any of these young men here him to greet.
But trusting he will ever find your temperance armor bright,
I bid you a kind farewell and a pleasant good-night.

THE TEMPERANCE CAUSE.

LADIES AND GENTLEMEN: I suppose you have assembled here to hear something in behalf of the temperance cause, and I sincerely hope you will not be disappointed in your expectations, if you only hear a little, as it will be that much good done. For by the combination of small things great and glorious objects are often achieved, and without unity there can no good be accomplished. Then let us unite in one of the great and grand causes of our country. Let us embrace every opportunity whilst it is within our reach.

Just look, if you please, at our city and its vicious surroundings, caused by intemperance, one of the greatest curses of our land—for instance, the whisky houses and dram shops, satanic dens of vice, where all the false allurements of vain pleasures, in their most beautiful colors, are held out to the bewildering gaze of the thoughtless youth. Thus the artful tempter entraps them into his dreadful abodes of sin, and accomplishes his fiend= ish work of destruction. "Oh! fathers and mothers! where is your wonted influence over the youthful mind and heart?" Can not you stay the hand of the great destroyer, who numbers his victims by the thousands multiplied by thousands? Will you allow this great privilege to pass, when it is within your power to arrest it, and thus save your sons and daughters from the destructive influence of whisky?

Pause a moment! be very careful how you act; this is not a

mere trifle, but a matter of grave importance. "O, that you may never have to look back on this place with shame or repentance for the neglect of duty on your part, to your children. If you do, be assured that the golden opportunities you have let pass for them will then rise up against you, and be paid for by years of bitter regret." But God forbid that any here to-night should ever have cause of remorse in their action of duty. For how often are fond parents' hearts wrung with bitter anguish, "sorrowing their gray hairs are brought down to a premature grave." For what? Whisky and its evil influences. Then I say: Young man, look well to your footsteps; in an hour when you think not the demon may overtake you. Look you at the hundreds of young men whose prospects were as bright and promising as yours are to-night, who have went down in shame and disgrace and filled dishonored graves. And young ladies, you need to be interested in this cause. You have brothers, and some of you may possibly have some one that feels dearer than a brother to you, who are exposed to this great evil of mankind. Look over our surrounding country and see the broken-hearted wives whose prospects a few years ago were as bright and promising as yours are to-night.

But hark! hear you her sorrowful cries,
　　Calling on one whose heart is as stone?
See the drops of grief gushing from her eyes—
　　Her voice grows faint, her happiness is gone.

Her fair hand was wooed and won
　　By a youth of her playmate days,
A sister's pet, a fond mother's son,
　　But alas, now, how changed are his ways.

Her warm and tender heart
　　Has melted within her bosom.
She smiles and weeps when they part,

Shrinking back into love's prison.

And in this unholy land of care,
   She lingers her untimely life away—
The siren song of love has proved a snare,
   Her happiness to grief an unfortunate prey.

To her, love's young dream is o'er, and alas !
   Hope from her bosom has forever fled.
And ere the days of absence can pass,
   Love shall prove withered and dead.

In her visions fair her brightest joys have fled—
   All to her is a world of despair and gloom.
She may now well lay that crested head,
   And hang that broken heart o'er the tomb.

HOPE.

There is no word in our language more expressive than the little word hope. Every one hopes. All hearts are turned toward the radiant star, hope. It is the bright meteor that gives to the heart the faith which stands as a sure brace for the half ship-wrecked vessels of the heavenly saints. Yea, it is that oriental star which we see in this sombre world, as we mount on the silvery wings of faith to gain a home in heaven.

Oh ! bright and beautiful star of hope,
   We hail thee in thy glorious form,
We see thee as a speak at a distance remote,
   Beckoning to us in life's fearful storm.

The lowest human being on earth doubtless has a hope. Though the night be ever so dark, with hope in the palpitating heart, blazing up and enkindling genial warmth in the despair frozen bosom, mounts on the swift steed of untiring perseverance, and rides over the billowy-bosomed sea of life, surmounting the rugged waves that are perpetually heaving upon the tottering bark that is rapidly bearing us on to the further shore. 'Tis hope, that bright little star, which we see in yon dark-curtained future, surrounded with the murky clouds of despair, seems but a pale, glimmering spark afar, its brilliancy almost quenched by the unceasing showers of melting tears poured from the dismal clouds of grief and care. But as we are rapidly drifting down time's herculean stream, drawing nearer to the hidden realms of eternity, the lamp of life now nearly extinguished, it begins to brighten as the life-giving rays of hope beams with a crystaline light over the shrouded vale which hangs between us and the morrow.

As in youth, so when thy locks are thin and hoary,
It still reigns in thy bosom with all its glory.

HOME.

Home is one among the dearest words in our language, full of meaning and tenderness. The kindred ties of home lie nearest our hearts. For there we first found our sweetest associations, in childhood's innocence culled the sweets from every fragrant flower that grew by the wayside of life's early morning, sparkling with pearly gems of dew which we kissed from their shining leaflets. The word home is filled with so many precious memories. For there it was the first lessons in life were taught us by a fond and gentle mother, whose hallowed influence will follow us along the rugged paths of life, no matter how far from that loved home we be. The endearing words and loved scenes of home can never be forgotten. Home! what vast mul-

titudes bless that one loved word home! Who is it that does
not prize his home, you might well say his earthly heaven? For
there we possess all that is in this world dear to us, our best
friends and earthly treasures with them.

> Though our earthly treasures be small,
> With loved ones to heed our call,
> And their kind sympathies to cheer life's way,·
> Though the clouds be heavy and dark the day,
> With their kindly cheer our burdens are lighter,
> The clouds scatter and our days grow brighter.

> Home is where we have our sweetest pleasures,
> And all of life's richest treasures,
> Carefully stored away in safe-keeping,
> To nourish us whilst life is silently creeping,
> And when death shall come to claim his own,
> Then we shall gently pass over to our heavenly home.

But for the love of home, where is an individual who would
not undergo many hardships and trials to add joy and comfort
to their home? What is it that animates the the daily laborer
whilst toiling from early morn to dusky eve? 'Tis the hope of
adding comforts to his loved home. And what is it that stimu-
lates the untiring student, whilst sitting confined in his room,
deprived of the many sports in which he might have participated
that he loved so well, was he not thus employed? Why, it is
the love of home burning in his bosom, and the determination
of doing something to benefit himself and society. With this
noble purpose in view, his energies glowing with transport,
awakened by the fond aspirations of a happy home that he will
some day psosess, where he can can retire from the busy scenes
of the world, quietly to his own meditations, surrounded by
the comforts of life, and those whom his heart holds most dear,
to enjoy with him his gained treasures, as they gently glide

down life's stream together. Why is it that people are always striving to gain, as they cannot live always to enjoy it, neither take anything with them when they die? No, but they are striving to make and store up something for a home—why not happy homes? We should strive to cultivate our minds and affections, so that our homes may be happy, for—

> Wealth and luxury can not alone
> Make us a quiet and happy home.
> Nay, if we would have a happy home,
> One that our loved ones will not from it roam,
> We must surely in our bosoms ever cherish
> The diadem of love which can never perish;
> Whose lustre will but the brighter shine
> In the dark eventide of life's decline.

> Love is the sure foundation of a happy home,
> Without it home would only be a prison forlorn;
> Its inmates would soon abandon its walls
> To seek peace elsewhere 'midst pleasure's halls.
> No passion incidental to humanity embraces
> So vast a realm in life's ever-changing phases,
> As the varied forms of congenial love,
> Purifying the soul for the celestial courts above.

MAN'S CREATION.

Man is taught by nature the kind of a being he is, and what he was created for. God talks not to mortal man, neither visable nor invisable; but he unmistakably reveals his will to him through nature. For we might say that man, in his present form, is one of earth's natural plants, created for earthly purposes, so long as he remains in his present tabernacle. And it is by the close observance of all natural objects of nature that we are enabled to conceive a correct idea of what kind of creatures we are, for when we come to think of it minutely and investigate the subject of creation, we find there are a great many different kinds of creation, and that each and every one is created for its own purpose in nature. Yet some individuals seem to think (that is, they say) there is but one great, grand or universal creation ; they contend that man is no more than brute creation. If so why does not man, like other beasts of the field, content himself with his present existence, not fret nor worry about the future ? But it certainly is man's natural instinct to be a worshipping creature, and why should he be if there was no god to worship? For nature must undoubtedly be true to herself, and we learn from ancient historians that the heathen nations worshipped the heavenly planets for their god, when they had not so much as ever heard of a Supreme Being.

It undoubtedly is a natural instinct given to man by nature to teach him that there is a God, and a higher and nobler life for man to enjoy in the distant future somewhere, that this earth is only his temporary home, and, as a matter of fact, we can only enjoy earth as it is. We can only make ourselves happy and contented if we try, or we can drag out a miserable existence, if we choose. It altogether depends on our sense and ability as to whether we do well in this life or not, and it does seem to me to be a kind of superstition in people who hold to such ideas as fate decrees certain things to be, that could not be avoided nor helped, when in reality it originated in their own mismanagement or neglect.

For " Luck is pluck," I say.
" Where there's a will there's a way,"
And those who follow precepts true
Will make life a success all through.

16

'Tis our mistakes we make in life
That brings our care and strife,
For life lived practically is a scene
Of happiness and contentment, I ween.

WOMAN, THE WEAKER VESSEL.

Woman the weaker vessel, in an intellectual sense of the
word or phrase, is a query that has long been agitated in the
minds of a great many men of modern times, and it does seem
to my mind rather an illogical one, from the simple fact that the
world has long since conceded that woman's power is greater
than man's. And if woman be the weaker faculty, why does
she wield such an influence over man, the boasted lord of
creation? Man was doubtless created as a protective power for
woman, not a superior, and as such they have unmistakably
held their position, for woman, generally speaking, naturally
looks to man for her protection.

God, in his infinite wisdom, which is far beyond mortal
man's intelligence, created all things for definite purposes. And
that all things whatsoever he created should harmonize for the
good he intended, that nothing should go out void, nor return
unto him empty, that his purposes should not be defeated.
Therefore woman was created as man's helpmeet, (not help to eat,
as many seem to think) a pleasure and comfort for him. We
have divine authority for this word : God said it was not good
for man to be alone, therefore he made him a helpmeet. Not a
mere something to rule over, for he had created the beasts of
the fields, the flying fowls of the air, and the fishes of the sea,
and gave man dominion over them, but not woman. And now,
whilst man was monarch of all he surveyed, yet there was a

vacancy to be filled. God had not yet created his grand work of creation, and now, in his profound wisdom, performed his last and best creation when he made woman. And endowed her with the same intellectual powers of man, thereby fitting her for a suitable companion, a comforter, a solacer, and a pleasure for him, not a menial slave. It is surpassing strange, yet 'tis true, that most persons always take advantage of a thought or word in their own favor. For instance, the word or epithet commonly applied to woman as the weaker vessel, man generally attributes its meaning to woman's intelligence, when, indeed, it only refers to her physical creation.

Man is most assuredly, through the divine oracles, told to honor woman as the weaker vessel, not to look upon her as a shallow-brained imbecile, that would be a strange way to honor anyone. I beg to be excused, I ask no such honors at their hands. And would it not be more reasonable to suppose if man was endowed with superior intellect to that of woman he would very readily understand at once the meaning of the word, or phrase, weaker vessel, to refer to her physical developement, as it is clearly defined by all natural objects. For nature is true to herself in every respect, as there is not anything in nature or natural objects but what have their uses in the economy of nature, and for us to deny anything is so, only because it is beyond our feeble comprehension, is surely absurd, to say the least of it. And we clearly understand that the finer a piece of mechanism the weaker it is, and the coarser and rougher it is the stronger. So it is with man's creation, man being the first creation, created from the crude rudiments of the earth, whilst woman, being the last, finest and best creation, was taken from man after the refining process was completed in him ; hence she is called the weaker vessel.

So far as intellect is concerned, woman first attaine

knowledge and then gave it to man. Why, if he was so much her superior, did he accept it at her hands? Take the advice of a simpleton when he knew it was forbidden fruit, and thus incur the displeasure of his great Creator in disobeying one of His most positive commands? Why risk the fearful consequences, if he possessed so much wisdom? Hence 'tis conclusive to my mind that man and woman's intellect by nature and culture are equal, but woman's power is greatest.

IMPROVEMENT.

Improvement is one among the most progressive advance ments of the age. It is seen everywhere, swiftly tripping along the endless road of perfection, with its beneficial capacities disclosing its refined elegance in the advent of time, fulfilling the the duty assigned to its portion, as time rolls along the dark ages of eternity, in revealing as they pass the material events of future years. Improvement is one of the most extensive enterprises in the world. It expands throughout all our universe, completing the works of nature into a more perfect and beautiful state of scenery to the admiring gaze of man, thereby presenting to his mind a more lofty contemplation of the benevolence of Deity.

Improvement is one of the most essential works in existence, daily presenting itself to our view and manifesting the ability that was committed to it, showing forth the power and wisdom of an Infinite Being throughout the earth's remotest bounds. Unfolding her responsibilities into the arms of nature for a more extended space to complete in the rolling tide of years; adding more beauty and grandeur to our benighted world than any other acquirement, having produced a considerable change here in the last century. Where once was a dreary wilderness, infested with wild and ferocious beasts, inhabited by a wild and savage race, is now a peaceful, civilized and enlightened nation. Instead of wigwams and huts are now stately edifices arrayed in magnificent splendor; and the lone prairies which had nothing to ornament their valleys, save their green vesture, are are now dotted with animals of various kinds, sporting about as if proud of their station. Improvement is one of the most benificent works of creation, full of significance and power.

ALWAYS LOOK ON THE BRIGHT SIDE.

"Always look on the bright side of everything," is an old precept, and should be practiced by everyone. If people would only take care not to look on the shady side of life, there would be a great many more pleasant faces and cheerful voices. For imaginary troubles, in most all instances, are worse than real ones, as the coinage of the brain, to a considerable extent, is very lively, always in action, and will, in its fancies, present objects in a thousand different forms, whilst real troubles are natural and can, with fortitude and a firm resolution, be easily braved through.

To look on the bright side of everything should be an infallible rule, and observed by everyone, for there is scarcely anything in existence but what has two sides, shades, or colorings. For an instance, we will take the young student that is just entering on the stage of manhood. See him as he opens the great journal of his life and views, as it were, the first broad page of his futurity. He sees the dark clouds hovering around him, and, as far as the eye can penetrate, the vast realms ahead

of him seems one great plain, enshrouded with smoke and fog.
Now—

His fairy phantom boat, of ambition and hope,
On life's rugged waves, scarcely can float,
But is sinking underneath the billows of despair
When a sylph-like form, so beautiful and fair,

bids him turn the leaf and view the other side.   With utter
astonishment he beholds, at a great distance, a beautiful valley
all covered with the greatest variety of flowers and evergreens,
and through it a majestic river is flowing rapidly, bearing on
its broad bosom the finest vessels imaginable, drifting on to the
shoreless seas of eternity.   And whilst thus viewing the scene,
though at so great a distance, and contemplating what to do, his
bosom swells with emotion.   He is now filled with awe and
admiration at the divine works of an all-wise Providence, and
resolves to press onward.   But on looking around he sees those
dark, angry clouds still lowering and large mountains rising
before him, and his pathway intercepted with rugged precipices.
He now exclaims, "Alas! alas! there are too many obstacles in
the way.   It is vain, it is folly to think of such a perilous
journey."   And now, whilst his almost despairing heart sinks
within him, hope bids him look higher.   He looks, and now
beholds a different scene: he sees the fair fields of fame and
renown lying just beyond this beautiful valley, and, on making
a more minute examination of the picture, he discovers quite
a number of youths pressing onward to those elysian fields.
Some have reached the desirable place, others are nearly there,
and some just making their start.

   And now, whilst viewing life's beautiful picture, though
fraught with so many dangers and difficulties, his ambition is
fully aroused.   He now resolves to press onward, and always
look on the bright side of everything.

And now, dear young friends, remember that you are just starting out upon the journey of life and you should be very careful the course of action you take in early youth, as your future happiness, in a great degree, depends mostly upon the kind of impressions received and tactics practiced in your childhood. If you spend the bright morning of life in idleness and vain pursuits, you may be sure at eventide to meet with remorse and disappointment. And now, whilst life's morning so brightly dawns, press onward, look forward to the blazing star of hope, which, will guide you safely through the dark ages of futurity, throwing its sunlight o'er the shadowy paths that lie through the gloomy forests of the beyond. And if you meet with trials and disappointments, never despair; remember that our lives, like the tempestuous sea, sometimes smoothly glides, then again angry storms o'er her billows ride. So through the ever-changing scenes of life, always look on the bright side of everything.

CRANKS.

Cranks are a peculiar sort of people that are talked about a great deal now-a-days ; only because people know more about them now than they did in our grandmother's time. Of course there were not a few then called cranks who out-cranked those that so nick-named them ; but as a common rule those that are always so ready to call someone a crank are those over-wise, knowing things who are the worst of the two, yes, two to one the crankiest, for their knowledge of psycology is scarcely equal to that of the friendly mosquitoes, for they will probe through your dress to see what kind of stuff you are ; but these self-conceited parasites never look any further into a man than his dress

or external appearance.   'Tis not the individual, but the dress
that they esteem.

When you please the eye of a fool you tickle his vanity.
The only difference between a dude and a crank (what some
people call a crank) is that one is a fool for clothes, and the other
a fool for the lack of them.—

> Fine feathers for a fine bird,
>   Not for a man's much speaking,
> Will he in a crowd be heard,
>   For men's eyes are vainly seeking
> To please the eye, not the ear ;
>   For a witty fool in fine clothes
> Will they more willingly hear
>   Than a man who everything knows,
> And chooses for himself to wear
>   A costume of comfort and pleasure,
> Regardless of being called a bear,
>   Or hailed as a stylish treasure.

And these are the kind of people who, in an independent,
noble manner, dress and act to correspond with their nature and
good sense, and who are called cranks by the fashionable snob—

> Who sports a watch and chain,
>   And wears his broad cravat,
> Whilst with a fashionable cane
>   He tips his bee-gum hat.
> And, oh ! a young lady to meet,
>   What an all-glorious smile
> He'd give her on the street,
>   Her unwary heart to beguile.
> But he is only the chaff
>   Of society's true man ;
> And not the genuine staff

On God's true original plan.
So it matters not very much
What he says of anything, nor how;
For his gossip and all such
Doesn't amount to a good bow-wow.

MAN'S TRANSGRESSION.

Man's transgression brought to him sin, sorrow and death.
He died in order to gain wisdom; yea, he died in the purchase
of wisdom, in eating the fruit of the forbidden tree of knowledge.
Man fell from his purity by this transgression, and if he would
become truly wise he must now die to sin. As it was then with
man, he eat of the tree of knowledge to become wise; so it is
now, if he would gain the true wisdom which surpasseth all
understanding he must accept Christ (who is our tree of knowledge) and die to sin, if he would gain the only true wisdom and
be enabled to eat of the tree of life and live forever.

The tree of knowledge was put in the Garden of Eden for
man, doubtless, when he should arrive at the years of maturity
(not for children); then, at the proper time, in eating the fruit
of knowledge, they would have become wise as gods, hence they
would have been prepared to eat of the tree of life and lived
forever. But the fruit was unsuited for children, therefore God
commanded Adam and Eve not to eat of it (as they were but
children in knowledge at that time and only needed children's
food to nourish them until the proper time for strong food should
be required); that in the day they did eat of it they would
surely die. And as God created them he surely knew what was
best for them. But the children disobeyed their father and had
to be punished; justice demanded it. So, after they had eat of

the tree of knowledge and knew good from evil, God drove them out of the Garden of Eden, placing there a cherubim and flaming sword between them and the tree of life lest they might pluck it and live forever.

Christ is a type of this beautiful figure. Christ is our Tree of Life and Knowledge. If we accept Him and become enlightened we will then love Him and obey Him, and when we have passed over the sword of mortal death, which is between us and our God, we will then eat of the tree of life freely to the enjoyment of the soul's salvation, redeemed from under the curse of sin by the blood of the lamb.

As the tree of life and knowledge was planted in the Garden of Eden to be used at the proper time by man, and would have been a blessing had it not been plucked in the wrong season, thereby causing man to suffer in consequence of this untimely act; hence they have been transplanted to the Garden of Eden in Paradise. Now, Christ is our tree of life and knowledge, and if we would gain this true knowledge and live forever we must accept Christ and die to sin, and thus become enlightened, eat of the tree of life and live. For, as man was created in the beginning a pure being, in the image of his Divine Creator, and died through his transgression to gain knowledge, and thus become a slave to sin ; so now he must die to sin, and accept Christ, the tree of life and knowledge, to inherit salvation and to live forever.

Death is the sword placed between man and eternity ; as man is when the sword cuts him down, so eternity finds him. If he has part in Christ he is admitted to the tree of life, for he has passed over the sword of mortal death, where he can now eat of the tree of life freely which stands on either side of the beautiful river of life, its pure waters clear as crystal flowing from out the throne of God and the lamb, and inherit eternal salvation, purchased by the blood of the lamb for the atonement of man's sins ;

but if he has no part in Christ, passes over the flaming sword of death and inherits eternity, an eternal death of misery and despair.

Oh ! could we but lift the veil
    Which hides from our view eternity ;
See the world of woe, and hear the wail
    Of lost spirits who dwell in misery ;
See the hedious frown of dark despair
    Impressed upon the woe-begone feature
Of the once beautiful brov so fair,
    The lovely image of a seraphic creature,

Whose heart we had thought too pure,
    Too guiltless to ever enter there ;
    A world of vexation, sorrow and care,

Methinks this evil we would shun,
    A life more careful we would live,
And when each day's work was done
    Its toil would sweeter rest give.
For no bitter thoughts of injured friends
    Would disturb our peaceful slumber.
In living a life on which heaven depends
    Our every act would be a vital number.

Oh ! could we but lift the veil
    Which hides heaven from our view,
And see the crystal waters that never fail
    In the river of life for I and you,
And near its margin on either side
    Behold for us the beautiful tree
The lamb of God, our Savior crucified
    Has purchased for you and me,

Methinks our light afflictions here

Would make us appreciate heaven more,
For its beauties through them more clear
Would shine from the golden shore ;
And methinks on the wings of faith I see
In the bright, beautiful land of love
The dear ones who dwell in eternity
Spread their snowy wings in climes above
And soar away in other regions fair,
In the eternal light of God's love
To ever live and dwell there.

Then let us, dear friends, ever strive
In a fairer world than this to arrive,
Where sunlight nor heat never come,
But the weary cares of life are done.

THE GOOD OLD TIMES.

Why is it that we so often hear people speak of the good old times? Is it possible that in the ages of ignorance and superstition, times were better and more appreciated than in this enlightened age? Certainly not, but this evidently is only a fancy or whim which carry people back to their home associations of early life when its cup was overflowing with the fondest feelings and purest affection of home life; unmixed with sophistry and deceit, consequently those were their good times, hence, they say the good old times, and as the world progresses, those good old times will ever be cherished in fond memory from one generation to another for doubtless fifty years, hence, people will speak of to-day of their good old times. So far as the times are concerned, they are just what people make them. If we want good times, we must help to make them good. But how are we to do it? By doing right ourselves, and thus encouraging others to do so by our example, and discountenance those who persist in wrong-doing and possess immoral habits. Shun their society, thereby teaching them if they would be respected, that they must conduct themselves respectable. In speaking of the good old times, we all know that it is but natural for people to look on the early part of their lives, when their hopes were all in the future and their morning skies were unclouded with care, as their happiest days and good old times, e'en if they have been e'er so hard, their hardships would now have been forgotten. For as the years come and go by, and our future hopes have not been realized as our expectations had planned them out for us, of course our disappointments make us feel as though the times are not now what they once have been. Never has there been a time since the creation of the world, but what times have been hard with some portion of its inhabitants, especially the poor and afflicted, for Christ said : "The poor ye always have with you," and at any time you may help them. So the poor and afflicted we have had, and will doubtless always have among us. Then when we hear people speak of the good old times, we should only think that their burdens of life have been either lighter, or else they had more courage and fortitude to bear them than now ; that it was more in themselves than the times. I have often been amused when listening at the conversation of individuals meeting after a lapse of years, in relating the former days of their acquaintance, when in the good old times they enjoyed life so much better than now ; when they had no railroads, no telephones and but few telegraph wires, consequently, did not hear of half the crime that was committed in the country nor half of the want and destitution which prevailed among its inhabitants, and as a matter of fact in such instances, "ignorance is bliss," for they could not realize anything of which they knew nothing of. Therefore, those were their happiest days and good old times. But now how changed are the times ; they can hear from all parts of the world in a few days, instead of months and years, which brings the tragic story of death, of famine, pestilence and destitution to them every day from some portion of the world. Wherefore, this is an evident fact to their minds, that the world grows more wicked instead of wiser and better, and it is really diverting to hear them speak of the hard old times, when they had to grind their bread with a steel mill turned with (not by) a crank, and how sweet the coarse corn-bread eat, and its being ground coarse made it so much more digestible ; and how much better and nicer the flavor of coffee was, when parched in a large oven with a lid over it, around an old fashioned fire-place, and those old-fashioned sweet-potatoes (not the improved) was so much nicer when baked in an oven around the fire-place. They were so juicy, and in fact, everything seemed more substantial, because it took such hard labor to produce it. They certainly thought it must be better than these new-fangled ways of modern inventions, with which, by a simple but effectual process, we can cook a whole meal in a few minutes with but a small handful of wood, or even none at all ; for it seems so easy done that they think it can't be as good as the old way.

As good as the old way,
  When women over the fire,
Baked their brains day by day,
  To cook a meal for their sire.
And I can well remember
  When a cook-stove was introduced,
Into a household, every member
  With the greatest anxiety was induced

To behold the great invention,
  Which was woman's burden to lighten,
And give her toilet more attention
  - Wherewith her sire's face to brighten.

And it certainly did, for awhile,
  Prove a grand household joy,
In bringing to it many a smile
  To bless ; instead of a frown to annoy.

But, like other devices, wrought
  By the skilled art of man,
When ingenuity had brought
  Finer inventions on a better plan,
The original but a shadow of the new,
  Lost its magic charm so dear,
And has become so common too,
  That 'tis no longer music for the ear.

For the desires, or inward cravings of man, like the restless
ocean wave that is continually surging, is never at rest, but is
ever reaching out in its research into the mysterious labyrinths
of the future for fields of investigation wherein they may attain
a more thorough knowledge of their creation and its purposes.
And it is truly wonderful the rapid strides which man has made in
scientific researches within the last half-century.   I say half
instead of a whole century, because a great many people can look
back within their own individual knowledge over this stretch of
time, and can realize its progress much better than if referred
back a century to ponder over the read-knowledge gleaned from
different writers.   For that which is seen with thine own eyes is
far better understood and realized than the history given from
the views of others, as we can't see all things alike, and the same
scenes often draw out entirely different feelings and expressions
from different individuals.   Hence, the differences of opinion
that originate in the human family arise from this source, as
but few people are constituted alike ; what might please some,
perhaps would disgust others ; therefore, the creation of man,
when we take into consideration the millions of inhabitants,
occupants of the same world, subject to a like condition in life,
yet so different in understanding in the whole sense of the word,

is the grandest mystery of earth.   Man can, and will solve
many things of this earth which seems now a mystery to him.
For many things appear mysterious to us, when, in fact, 'tis no
mystery—only our misapprehension—but man can never the
mystery of his own creation understand only in part, until he
passes through all the different stages of his existence, which will
doubtless lead him through other worlds than this, then when he

Reaches that wonder-land
  On the further shore,
Will he, on the golden strand,
  E'er sigh for the days of yore ?
Will the good old times
  E'er be cherished there,
When heaven's melody chimes
  Softly and sweetly everywhere
In a fairer land of love,
  Where no false friendships deceive ?

O, then, think not of the past,
  As the good times of yore,
But let our anchor be cast
  Leeward bound to a fairer shore.
Then our good times will begin,
  When we've passed from earth away,
When we cease to mourn for sin,
  And chant redemption's sweet roundelay.

Yes, our good times will be,
  When we on the silvery strand,
Meet the loved ones we've longed to see
  And join their sweet seraphic band
To rejoice in the light of eternal day,
  Where the gloom of sorrow's night
Ne'er throws its shadows o'er the way,
  Nor veils the joys of Heaven's light.

And sweet will that welcome be
  From the loved ones gone before,
To share with them bright eternity,
  Where earth's cares come no more.

But in Heaven's beautiful clime,
No tempests ever wreck the sky,
Nor sunset, at latest eve's decline,
Immortality can never fade nor die.

FAREWELL.

What a feeling of sadness this word brings to us, especially when we are called upon to take a final departure from dear friends. 'Tis then we realize the sadness of this lonely word. And yet the word farewell we may at any time see and hear in the grand arena of nature's universe, for it is beautifully written on the fading flowers of earth, as they pass from the stage of existence. Their beauty and lovliness, as they fold their leaves in death, say farewell. It is written

On the golden leaves
Of the forest trees,
As they rustle in the evening wind,
And gently to the ground descend,
Twirling 'round in a magic spell,
Say, farewell, farewell.

The sweet little bird, perched upon a limb, singing its song so free, unplumes its wing and soaring away, says farewell. The golden sun, as it sinks beneath the horizon, its lingering rays shimmering and fading from view, says farewell. The closing day, in her gentle twilight's fall, with the softest accent of eve's latest zephyr, whispers farewell. The stars in silence that shed their soft silvery light, as they gently pass their onward course, say farewell.

So shall all earth's inhabitants say;
Whether by thought or action expressed,
Farewell, as their days pass away,
And their youth in sable garments are dressed.

For earth and all of its creatures are
   But passing shadows beneath the sky;
Which appear as a wandering star
   Twinkling in the misty realms afar.

For this is but the shadow land
   Of the beautiful beyond in eternity bright,
Where, from the surf-beaten strand
   Of eternal shores, the material light

Throws the shadows of substance behind,
   Revealing in that glorious world above
Earth's mysteries, to the opening mind
   Of man, the great light of God's love.

And tho' our friends oft say farewell,
   'Tis only a wish of kindness expressed ;
A feeling of tenderness to tell—
   Only a departure's pleasing address.

For the word farewell, like many others, is varied in its meaning, and is often misconstrued and frequently misapplied, for the lack of knowing its true and original significations. For if we will examine this word carefully, we will find that a great many people use it in a vague sense, as the word "farewell" is a compound word composed from the two words, fare, and well. By the word fare, we understand that to signify a state or condition ; and it may be either good or bad ; and the word "well" signifies something similar only used in a more positive sense, as it always conveys the same idea to the mind. If we say 'tis well, we know it to be good. Then farewell does not always convey to the mind a feeling of final separation when used in its proper sense ; but as a kind wish expressed ; that the fare or condition in which you may be placed might be good or well, as may you fare well, that is, may your condition be good, so I say farewell gentle reader.

   May life be pleasant with you.
   May its days unclouded with care,

Be spent in wisdom's ways so true
That no cloud can ever enter there.

May you the ages gently pass down,
    Safely moored on life's rugged stream,
Bear the cross and win the crown,
    Where its stars in eternity will gleam.

May your day dreams of life
    Be fill'd with a zealous love
Ever free from care and strife,
    For the work of thy Master above.

And tho' the dark clouds lower,
    And thy pathway here be dark,
And the pleasures of life seem o'er,
    Fear not, for you'll safely embark
At last on the shining shore.

VALEDICTORY SONG.

[RESPECTFULLY DEDICATED TO THE READERS OF THIS BOOK. E. F. P.]

When our bark drifts o'er life's raging sea,
And we land on the bright shores of eternity,
When the rugged waves of life's sorrows are crossed,
And in the joys of Heaven are forever lost.

We will hear the golden bells ringing,
We will hear the angel voices singing
When we meet again "on the shining shore,"
Where death, sin and sorrow come no more.

When the toils of earthly life are done,
And the glad victory o'er death is won,
When our spirits, freed from this mortal clay
Will bask in the light of eternal day.

We will hear the golden bells ringing,
We will hear the angel voices singing,

When we meet again "on the shining shore,"
Where death, sin and sorrow comes no more.

When we lay our bodies down to sleep
In silence, where none ever wake to weep,
When life's fierce battles with sin are o'er,
And we, with the saints, our Savior adore.

We will hear the golden bells ringing,
We will hear the angel voices singing
When we meet again "on the shining shore,"
Where death, sin and sorrow come no more.

O, come, ye weary pilgrims, burdened with care,
Look to Jesus.   He will your burdens share,
For He has gone before us ; mansions to prepare ;
That with Him we may forever dwell there.

Where we'll hear the golden bells ringing,
And hear the angel voices singing,
When we meet again " on the shining shore,"
Where death, sin and sorrow comes no more.

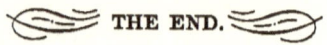 THE END.

www.ingramcontent.com/pod-product-compliance
Lightning Source LLC
Chambersburg PA
CBHW060611030726

47498CB00005B/1639